EXCEPTIONAL

BOOK ONE

by

Jess Petosa

D0967486

Dedicated to Brooke & Molly, for being my shining lights

And to BoSh, for pushing me further than I ever thought I could go.

Table of Contents

Prologue

In the year 2022, the United States government began experimenting with gene mutations. They set up a lab in South America and hand picked a team of scientists to work on the project. Their primary objective was to create a serum that would enhance the skills of a special ops team in the military, hopefully by way of strength and speed. In 2024, they would succeed in creating an injection of just this type. They called it SS-16. SS standing for Super Serum and 16 standing for the number of attempts it took to succeed.

What they would not foresee was that the serum they had created would evolve the human DNA past the desired result. At first it appeared to work as expected; the men were faster and stronger than any other humans in the world. But strange things started happening in the weeks that followed. One man burst into flames in the middle of the night, and when his squad was finally able to put the fire out, they found him unharmed. Another man found that he could move objects short distances just by pointing his hands at them.

The squad was quarantined on the base as the scientists attempted to figure out what had gone wrong, but one by one the scientists started to exhibit symptoms similar to what the soldiers had. Blood work showed that the scientists had the same genetic code as those who had been injected with SS-16. It was then that they realized they had created not just a super serum, but also an airborne virus.

By the time these conclusions were drawn it was too late. Others across the base were exhibiting symptoms of SS-16 and several had already left to travel home to the states. The virus spread like wildfire and was quickly labeled a pandemic by the World Health Organization.

There were no remedies for the sickness, or suggestions for avoiding infection. Leaders around the world told civilians to settle in and prepare for the worst, each hoping that somehow their countries would be passed over by the virus.

In the end, no country, city, or town was overlooked. A good portion of the world's population died in the first year because their bodies rejected the change, and enough had perished that the human race became an endangered species. Of the survivors, more than half were found to be immune. Their bodies never changed and their genetic work up came back SS-16 free.

One scientist was able to create a vaccine before the virus took his life, having worked day and night through the pain of the change. The vaccine suppressed the genetic mutation of the virus and held it at bay, as long as the infected human being took it once, by injection, every six months. The vaccine was easily reproducible and could have cured millions, but the infected caught wind and ordered the vaccine destroyed. In such a short time, they had already grown accustomed to their new strength and abilities, and refused to return to normal.

Governments broke down, countries lost communication, and entire cities fell to rubble from riots and misuse. Three U.S. cities remained standing in the end: Los Angeles, Chicago, and Philadelphia. But eventually no one would remember their names or what set them apart from other cities. All that had indentified these cities as what they were would be lost and forgotten.

The surviving infected, who would soon title themselves as Exceptionals, rebuilt with what they had left. They organized themselves into their own class and settled into the cities, getting the electric factories and other important businesses back up and running. Together, they learned to control their new abilities and use them in ways that would help advance their new society. They grew taller and stronger, and if anyone had doubts about someone being Exceptional, they could just look at a person's eyes. All Exceptionals had violet eyes. The strongest Exceptionals rose into leadership positions, while the others settled into intermediate jobs that were still vital to making the cities run.

As for the immune—who were now titled Ordinarys— they were banished to the suburbs to farm, make textiles for the cities, or even work in the production of steel and lumber. Some were given homes within the cities and hired on to do meager jobs like janitorial and cooking work. Life picked up a normal pace and despite the obvious separation between the Exceptionals and Ordinarys; everyone managed to live in peace. Slowly, the population began to increase and the fate of the country no longer looked dismal.

But as time passed things became dangerous for the Ordinarys. In the Midwestern City, a new Exceptional leader came into power a century and a half after the release of SS-16. He increased watch over the Ordinarys, placing Exceptional Guard patrols in each settlement to insure that adequate work was being done. Fifteen years into his reign, he enacted the Ordinary Volunteer Program. It allowed the Exceptionals to come to each settlement outside the City once a year and gather volunteers of teenagers and young adults. It was said that these groups of Ordinarys were taken into the City and were placed into new jobs, being given a better life then they had in the settlements. If no one volunteered for the task, the Exceptionals would be allowed to gather Ordinarys against their will, and bring them into the City by force.

There were always enough volunteers from each settlement though, since most Ordinarys grew up with a fierce curiosity about the City. No one questioned the law, and no one questioned the City leader. They knew one thing for certain; once an Ordinary entered the City, they never returned.

Chapter One

175 A.V.

"Ally, Wait up!"

Ally paused in a clearing, listening to the sound her brother made as he crashed through the brush behind her.

"Stosh, wild hogs would make less noise than that. This is why I wanted to leave you home."

Stosh shot her an irritated look. "If you didn't move so fast, I wouldn't have to crash through trees to catch up with you."

He took a moment to pick pine needles out of his hair. Dark locks fell into his eyes as his hands searched the remainder of his heavy mop.

"Besides, I don't see why we have to be so quiet. We aren't hunting, and we are no where near the boundary."

Ally lowered her voice. "It's caravan day."

Stosh's mouth fell open. "I forgot. And you dragged me out into the woods. Mother would kill you if she knew."

"I know. I just want to watch."

Stosh crossed his arms over his chest. "You've seen the caravan once a year for the past seventeen years, Al."

"Yes, but only from right outside of our home. I want to see what it looks like once it has already collected from a settlement. Don't you?"

He threw his hands in the air and walked toward the dirt road that lay a few yards to the north. "Where will we watch from?"

Ally looked upward. "The trees."

TEN MINUTES LATER they were situated twenty feet off the ground in a strong oak tree. Amazingly, they were able to find a branch that would hold both of them. Stosh had suggested that they choose separate trees so that if one of them was spotted, they wouldn't both be in trouble. But Ally waved him off.

"We aren't technically doing anything wrong," she pointed out.

"Then why are we hiding?"

"In case they decide they could use a few more Ordinarys."

"Good point," Stosh said as he looked down at the ground.

"Here they come." Ally pointed up the road where a black truck was headed toward them. A dozen Exceptional guards flanked it, their military grade guns held out in front of them.

She never got used to the sight of the Guards from the City. They were all Exceptionals and rumored to be bred into their position, standing at least 7 feet tall with their muscular bodies and violet eyes. There were also rumors that they had night vision, could see for over a mile, and could hear at twice the volume level that an Ordinary did. Ally believed it all.

The back of the truck was open so as it passed below them, Ally could make out the dozen Ordinarys within. They were sitting in a semi-circle, their backs pressed up against the sides of the truck. Some were laughing with their neighbor, probably friends that had volunteered with them. A few stared off into the woods, their gazes distant. Some Ordinarys left the settlements due to abusive families, loneliness, or pressure from others. Ally wondered if anyone ever truly regretted it and tried to take back the choice they had made before arriving at the entrance into the City. The Exceptionals would never let them return to the settlement. Volunteering was absolute.

When she and Stosh were younger, they used to play a game where they pretended they lived an extravagant life in the City. She was always an Exceptional, and Stosh was her Ordinary cook. He acted overly sensitive to her touch, since she was supposed to be unbelievably strong, and gave in to her every wish and command. Sometimes she would offer him the part of Exceptional, but he never took her up on it. He always told her that she played the part too well for anyone else to do it. Ally had thought more than once about volunteering, and had come very close when the last caravan came through, but her mother and Stosh needed her here.

After the caravan moved on, and they were sure that the Exceptionals were far away, she and Stosh climbed down the tree carefully.

"I wonder what settlement that was. Could you make out their markings? I think we were too high up." Stosh brushed dirt off his pants. "And another thing, if their senses are so superior, wouldn't they have realized we were up in the trees?"

"Do you ever wonder what it would be like to live in the City, Stosh?" Ally ignored his questions.

"Not this again," he said as he rolled his eyes. "I don't think it is as grand as they say, or wouldn't we all go?"

Ally shrugged. "They limit the amount of volunteers they take each year, so not everyone could go, even if they wanted to. Plus, no one comes back to tell any stories about the City, so we don't even know what it is like."

"Exactly."

"Don't you at least think it would be an interesting place to live?"

11

"I like where we live now." Stosh stomped off in the direction of their settlement, leaving Ally standing in the soft underbrush of the tree.

WHEN THE CARAVAN came through a settlement, the Ordinarys were required to sit inside their homes and wait for an Exceptional to come inside and ask for any volunteers. The process could take a few hours, and no one was permitted to step outside until the caravan had left the settlement. It wasn't until that evening that they discovered who had volunteered to leave for the City.

The caravan had come through Ally and Stosh's settlement several months ago, so they had more than half a year before it came back. Ally and her best friend had made a pact that they would volunteer that year, the year of their eighteenth birthdays. But when the Exceptional came into their home, Ally could feel Stosh's eyes boring a hole through the back of her head. He knew what she was about to do and that alone made her hold her tongue. Later that night, she found out that her best friend had volunteered, and Ally realized that she had betrayed her. Ally had said that she would volunteer, and now her best friend had gone into the City alone.

Ally caught up with Stosh and they jogged the one-mile distance back to the settlement. As they drew closer, the familiar scent of roasted meat filled the air, making Ally's stomach rumble. She hadn't eaten lunch today since she had been so focused on finding the caravan. She hadn't even been sure that it would be there, but she had heard stories from some of her older friends who claimed they had watched it pass from above. The caravans always came through on the first Monday of each month.

This was also the day that the City allowed the settlements to keep

12

a certain amount of extra meat to cook for a feast. It was said to be a thank you from the Exceptionals for the settlements allowing some of their own to move to the City. But some of the elder Ordinaries called it hogwash, a word that Ally always giggled at as a little girl. They said that Exceptionals didn't care enough to say thank you to the Ordinarys, and that there was something else going on with the volunteers. Ally's neighbor, Mr. Ryde, said that the Ordinarys were no more than cattle to the Exceptionals. Easy to herd around, butchered when necessary, and easily reproduced. Stosh thought that he was borderline insane.

"There you two are!" Their mother hurried toward them just as they stepped onto the packed dirt road that ran through the settlement.

"Stosh, you are needed with the wood cutters. The fire is getting low. Allona, come; let me brush out your hair." Their mother looked Ally over. "You were climbing trees again, weren't you?"

Ally's mother shuffled her off toward their home while Stosh took off in the opposite direction. Their settlement had once been a private neighborhood of some sort; at least that is what their ancestors had called it. Many of the houses were in ruins, but others had been maintained and inhabited by the remaining Ordinarys. The houses were modest and just enough for what they needed. Each home held two to three families, and in total there were over a hundred homes in their settlement. There were other settlements dotted along the suburbs of the City, packed tightly with people. Some Ordinarys dwelled far from the settlements, in what was called the Wilderness, but by doing that they gave up the right to have help from the Exceptionals in times of need.

"Look at your hair," Ally's mother said as she grabbed a brush from the drawer. "Let's see what I can do with this mess."

She worked quickly but gently through the knots in Ally's hair.

"Mother."

"Yes?"

"Stosh and I saw a caravan pass today." Ally made sure to leave out the part about how they had *purposely* found a caravan to watch.

The brush paused in her hair for a moment and she could see her mother's expression tighten in the stained mirror.

"You should have walked away, Allona."

"I wasn't going to volunteer."

"I know," her mother responded. Somehow Ally didn't believe that she did.

"There." Her mother patted her shoulder. Ally's long, dark hair now hung in soft waves down her back, stopping just at her elbows. She caught a glimpse of herself in the mirror. She had the same moss colored eyes as her brother and the same high cheekbones. While Stosh was on the thicker side from his time spent chopping trees in the woods, Ally was leaner. She had tightly packed muscle from her days of climbing trees and running through the woods, but her job as food gatherer didn't leave her much room for bulking up.

"Now go wash your hands and change your clothes for the feast."

Ally stood and walked down the hall to the room she shared with her mother. Their house had four bedrooms and they shared it with one other family: a mother, father, and two little girls. Generally, the sets of parents had their own rooms and then the same sex children each shared a room, but Ally hadn't wanted to sleep in the same room with the little girls. Since her father hadn't been around since Ally was born, her mother had no issue sharing a room with her.

She changed into a simple pair of black pants and a black long sleeved shirt. They made their own clothes here in the settlement, with textiles they bought from the city. Everyone wore similar outfits day by day, except for those who wore special uniforms for their occupations. It was said that there was once a day when people had whole rooms full of clothes and shoes. Dresses, pants, and all sorts of things. Now the only time men and women dressed up was on their wedding day. Each civilian had three pairs of pants, three pairs of shirts, and three pairs of undergarments to call their own. Some women would sew extra clothes with left over fabric and make a dress or a billowy skirt, but the desired effect went unnoticed. It was easier to work and function in pants.

Stosh returned an hour after he was sent to chop wood, announcing that the feast would begin in a little over an hour.

"They were almost completely out of wood. I have no idea what Po would do with out me," he said with a grin.

The City appointed one man from each settlement to step into a leadership role, rotating someone new in every ten years. Po had been chosen to run their settlement four years ago, and had proven to be a wise and efficient leader. Their main output for the City was wood, so he made sure that production ran smoothly and set-up the times for the City to receive their shipments. There were talks that Stosh would be his successor one day, since Po had no sons of his own. That was another reason Ally believed Stosh would never willingly go to the City.

"Want to go for a run through the woods?" Ally asked as Stosh plopped down next to her on the sofa.

"Didn't we just do that?" he asked.

"Yes," she smiled.

"What are you up to?"

"I was thinking." Ally picked at a frayed seam on the sofa.

"Maybe today we could jump the boundary. We're going to be eighteen tomorrow and almost *everyone* has jumped it before eighteen."

"No way." Stosh looked disgusted that she had even mentioned it. He was such a rule follower. "Not on caravan day. More Exceptionals will be patrolling the woods."

"Oh come on. Tomorrow you can brag to your friends about how you stepped over the boundary. It is almost a right of passage!"

Ally couldn't help but be enthusiastic. She had always wanted to take that fateful leap over the boundary line but had wanted Stosh to be the one to go with her. Of course there were risks involved. If she was caught by an Exceptional, she would be in big trouble. But no one was ever caught, and even if the Guards were near by, they didn't have time to mess around with silly Ordinary games.

"I'm going whether you go or not," she said, standing and walking toward the door.

"Fine," Stosh said.

Ally could tell by his body language that he was really annoyed with her. He would probably seethe about it until they got home, and then in the morning would recall how he hadn't had such an interesting night in awhile.

"That's the brother I know and love." She looped her arm through his, leading him out of the house and into the woods.

Chapter Two

The walk to the boundary line was about twenty minutes, which gave them just enough time to do the jump and then run back to the settlement for the feast. Their mother was helping the other women prepare for the feast, so she hadn't even been home when they left the house. She probably wouldn't even realize they had gone as long as they weren't overly late for the meal; and as long as Ally managed to keep her recently brushed hair unknotted. They took the familiar path through the woods and walked a good portion of the trip in silence.

"Were you planning on doing this with Willow?" Stosh spoke up when they were finally nearing the boundary line.

Ally froze in her tracks, focusing her gaze on the tree in front of her. Since it was summer the sun would not completely set for another hour or two, but it had already started its decent and was washing the woods in a beautiful orange glow.

"Why would you ask that?" Her voice was more of a breath.

After a few moments of silence Stosh spoke again. "Sorry."

She pointed to a large tree marked with a purple X. Someone from the settlement had marked it long ago and every year someone would paint over it again, making sure weather or other hazards didn't wash it away. This meant that they would step off the path and head down the slope toward the boundary line, which was less than a hundred yards away.

"Are you sure you want to do this?" Ally glanced back at Stosh, trying to forget his previous question. "You can back out at any moment."

Stosh rolled his eyes. "I'm not the downer you always make me out to be. We are here now, let's get this over with so that we aren't late to the feast."

He brushed past her and stepped around the marked tree, moving carefully as the ground sloped down. The boundary line was actually a small creek, small enough that with a running leap you could jump from one side to the other. Hence the term *jumping the boundary line*. As far as they could tell, the creek ran around the whole perimeter of the city limits. In order to reach the crowded suburbs and bustling City there was still a good mile or so to walk.

"I can see it," Stosh whispered to her. There was always an unspoken rule of being quiet around the boundary line.

Ally had been so focused on watching where she stepped that she bumped right into Stosh when he suddenly stopped in the middle of the path.

"St…" She stopped speaking mid-word when he raised a hand to silence her.

She peered around his body and saw what made him stop. Three boys stood on the other side of the creek, forming a semi-circle and talking in hushed voices.

"Dang," Ally whispered. Even though plenty of Ordinarys had jumped the boundary before, it was always considered insulting if someone arrived and did it right before you did, and then were still there to take jabs at you about it.

The boys were dressed in a muted gray color, which meant they were not from her settlement. Ally had heard other settlements received different color textiles to make their clothes, but she had no idea which one they might be from. At this distance, she couldn't tell what markings were on their wrists. They appeared to be her and Stosh's age, and well built. They could easily pass as woodcutters. One of the boys turned slightly toward the creek and Ally could tell he was grinning. He took one step back and then ran forward three strides before leaping over the creek. She cocked her head in confusion. You were only supposed to leap across the boundary, and then step back across. It symbolized the excitement of taking the risk and the shame of crossing back because you knew you didn't belong on the Exceptional side.

The boy stuck his landing and for added effect he dropped to one knee and placed one hand on the ground in front of him, and stretched the other out behind him. At that moment he raised his head, suddenly noticing Stosh and Ally. She would have realized it sooner had she *really* paid attention to the boy that had jumped through the air. The buzzed head. The precision of his jump. The grace with which he landed. And the violet eyes…

"Exceptionals," Stosh whispered.

He turned and tried to push Ally backward, but she stood her ground.

"No, not until I've made the leap."

The other two Exceptionals landed beside the first boy and stood on either side of him. Ally had never seen an Exceptional that wasn't a Guard, except for the posters of the City leader. They were still taller than an average Ordinary, but they didn't seem threatening at all. Their violet eyes threw her confidence off for a moment, but the boys didn't appear to pose any danger.

Ally stepped around her brother and started toward the creek.

The first boy to jump over the boundary line came and stood by her side, facing the creek with her.

"Are you sure you want to do this?" His voice was much gentler than she was expecting. The Exceptional Guards had such deep, rough voices. This boy sounded just like any Ordinary boy she had spent time around.

"More then ever." Ally glanced at him quickly before turning back to the creek.

He had the same standout violet eyes of the other Exceptionals, his buzzed hair looked thick and dark, and his facial features were very well defined. He stood almost a foot taller than her, but considering the Guards had at least two feet on her, this felt somewhat normal.

Ally could feel his gaze on her as she prepared to make the leap. She focused on the Exceptional side of the creek, which had been worn down and trampled from years of Ordinarys making the jump. They chose this spot because it was where the creek was at its narrowest, making for an easy crossing

"Will you stop staring at me?" she huffed at the Exceptional.

"Just waiting to see if you chicken out." He crossed his arms over his chest and took on a more relaxed stance. The gesture made Ally furious for some reason. She didn't normally get so worked up around boys, but this one set her mood on fire.

Her hesitation seemed to raise the boy's amusement in her. He let out a small laugh and then walked toward the creek, stepping through the shallow water and onto the other side. The two boys he came with did the same. They all turned to face her and stared for a long moment before taking off into the woods at a jog.

Stosh stepped up beside her and put a hand on her shoulder.

"Who should go first?"

Ally shrugged his hand off. "Me."

She stepped back and got a running start toward the creek. When she reached the edge she leaped into the air and landed with a *thud* on the Exceptional side, the heels of her boots just touching the edge of the water.

"Ha!" Ally yelled out, hoping the boys heard her as they jogged through the woods.

She turned to face Stosh, who was staring at her with his mouth open wide. He almost looked like he was in shock, which made her wonder if he had expected she would chicken out.

"Stosh, hurry up and get over here so we can go home. We wasted enough time on those Exceptionals."

Stosh continued to stare and very slowly raised his hand from his side, pointing at something behind her. Ally expected the Exceptional boys to be standing behind her, back to jab at her for something, like the length of her jump. But when she turned around she came face to face with two Exceptional Guards. More like face to ribcage since the Guards were so tall. She turned and ran toward the creek, trying to get to the other side, but two hands grabbed her from behind and threw her to the ground.

She rolled to her back and stared up at the two Guards. They were impossible to tell apart, which frightened her even more. One of them leaned over and sneered down at her.

"Ordinarys are not permitted on this side of the boundary line," his unnaturally deep voice growled at her.

Ally tried a plea of innocence. "I'm sorry, sir. I stopped at the creek to get a drink of water and saw a rabbit on this side. I thought I might be able to catch it if I snuck up on it. Please, I meant no harm."

The Guard laughed.

"I don't care *why* you are over here. It only matters that you are. You are now in the custody of the City, and you'll be coming with us."

Ally's breath caught in her throat. She had always thought that if they caught you, you would receive a warning and were sent home. She had never expected that they would actually take her into custody.

"No!" Stosh yelled from the other side of the creek, making his presence known for the first time.

The Guard's head whipped up. "Quiet Ordinary. Be grateful you are on the correct side of the boundary, or we would take you as well."

Ally watched in horror as her brother ran toward the creek.

"Stop!" she screamed, the desperation in her voice causing him to halt mid-run. The front of this boots splashed in the creek water. "Please. Don't. Go home to mother, Stosh, go home."

She swallowed back the lump that was growing in her throat. Stosh ran his hands through his hair in frustration, hard enough that Ally was sure he pulled clumps of it out. He paced for a few moments and then cursed, turning and sprinting back up the hill and into the woods.

She breathed a sigh of relief, but that relief was short lived as one of the Guards grabbed on to her hair and yanked her to her feet. Without another word they took their place on either side of her and marched her forward into the woods. Ally could see the big bridge through the trees, which meant the main road was up ahead. The bridge stretched over an area of the creek that was at least ten times the width of the spot they were at now.

They walked for ten minutes before the large military truck came into view. Ally could see several more Guards standing at attention around it, but despite their rigid posture, their expressions made them appear bored. She wondered if this was the same truck that passed underneath her earlier.

"Hey, wait!" a voice called from behind them.

The Guards spun around and since their hands were on each of Ally's arms, she ended up facing the same direction as them. The boy from the boundary line stood several yards in front of them, his friends on either side of him.

The Guard to Ally's right sighed and rubbed his head with his large, calloused hand. "What are you doing out here Lukin?"

She recognized that tone. It was the same tone she used with Stosh when she questioned the method with which he chose to do simple tasks, or when he crashed through the woods loudly on hunting days. This Guard knew this boy personally somehow.

"She's mine," the boy said as he pointed at Ally. "I claimed her."

The Guard eyed Ally carefully. "This one?"

The boy just nodded.

"How did she end up at the boundary? And with another Ordinary?"

"I didn't say I claimed her under normal circumstances."

There was a pause as the Guard glared at the boy. Ally had never seen such a furious face. The boy didn't stand down though, but instead stepped forward and put a possessive hand on her shoulder.

"Very well." The solider pushed her forward and the boy grabbed her arm. He dragged her back to his friends, keeping a tight hold on her.

"In front of the caravan, Lukin. Now," the Guard growled.

His friends took the lead and the boy that held her arm pulled Ally to the front of the truck, putting a decent distance between them and vehicle.

"Just follow my lead," the boy whispered in her direction.

A moment ago she had been afraid he would turn out to be as mean as the Guards that had taken her at the creek, but the tone of his voice had a soothing quality to it. Could he possibly be trying to help her out of this situation? Perhaps once they were near the City, the caravan would pass through and he would let her go.

Ally stopped this thought process. Stosh always said that she had a weakness toward wishful thinking, and he was right. Once they had gained a good distance on the caravan, which had apparently stopped to give the Ordinarys on board a bathroom break, the boy and his friends relaxed a little.

"What's your name?" the boy who had claimed her, whatever that meant, asked.

"Ally," her answer came out as a squeak. She looked down at her hands and realized that they were shaking.

"Ally." The boy repeated. "I'm Luke, and this is Pax and Maver." He motioned to the boys beside him.

The boy immediately to his right looked almost bald, his hair was such a fair color. Ally couldn't even be sure he had eyebrows. He was taller than Luke and despite his lean frame; he had plump cheeks that reminded her of the toddlers back in her settlement. He gave her a slight nod and a smile. The boy at the end had dark hair like Luke's, but his features were much different. He had a round face, almond shaped eyes, and pale skin. He avoided Ally's gaze, outwardly annoyed by her presence.

"Which settlement do you come from?" Luke asked.

"Oakwood," Ally responded, wondering if it was smart to hold a conversation with these boys, especially one that gave out any sort of information. She pulled back her sleeve and showed them the marking on her wrist. The Ordinarys in her settlement were all marked with the image of a large Oak tree. If she flexed the muscles in her arm, it almost appeared as though the branches were blowing in the wind.

It seemed impossible that just this afternoon she was sitting up in a similar looking tree with Stosh, watching a caravan pass below them. She should be back at the settlement, enjoying the feast with her family. Surely Stosh had made it back home by now and had told everyone what happened. She wondered if her mother was mourning right now, or maybe cursing her for being so ignorant. She hoped Stosh could hold the family together until she could get home. He had always been more fragile than her, more open to emotions. But that also made him great with support, and more understanding when it came to people's needs.

Ally spent the next twenty minutes watching her feet. Her black boots were worn down so much that it almost felt as if she were walking on the packed dirt with bare feet. The bottom of her pants had a rip in it, probably from walking through the woods to the creek, so she would need to have her mother repair it later that night. Again, hopeful thinking.

A clanging filled her ears and the faint smell of metal filled her nose. Ally lifted her head and fought the urge to gasp out loud. They had reached the City, and few hundred yards in front of them stood a two-story wall made of large stones. She had heard of the wall before, but never had it been described in this grandeur. It was said that the first generations of Ordinarys were forced to build this wall around the City, and that it took a full century to complete. Everything about it screamed *security* at Ally, and she was amazed that the boys she stood next to had even managed to escape the City. She knew that she would never be able to.

The clanging and metallic smell came from the machinery that was opening the large double doors that would give them entrance to the City. The doors were wide enough and tall enough that the caravan could pass through with ease. A dozen guards stood outside the door, and the number of them was probably more for effect as Ordinarys were brought in. Ally knew they were no real danger for the Exceptionals. Exceptionals were ten times stronger and faster than them all.

As they drew closer to the door, Luke took a firm grip on her arm. It was then that Ally realized she would not be released into the woods to run home. Luke and his friends were not here to aid her escape. Whatever claim Luke had on her, he meant to keep it. As they passed through the doors and into a stone tunnel, Ally closed her eyes and whispered out an apology to her family. She had a sinking feeling in her gut, one that told her she would never see outside these walls again.

Chapter Three

The afternoon had been as normal as any other for Luke. He and his friends were always looking for the next big adventure, and with their eighteenth birthdays and graduation looming before them; it was the perfect time to cross the boundary line. The idea had come from Pax's older brother, who had taken an Ordinary as his wife. She had told stories about how some Ordinary teens jumped the creek in the woods before their eighteenth birthday. It served as the boundary line between the Ordinary settlements and the City limit. While Ordinarys were forbidden to cross the line, Exceptionals were permitted to go back and forth as they pleased. That is, Exceptional Guards. Luke and his friends were not technically allowed to leave the City, but that hadn't stopped them.

What he hadn't expected was to run into the Ordinary girl and her male friend. At first he had just teased her as she prepared to jump the boundary line. It was obviously a much bigger deal to her than it would ever be to him and his friends. But after they had jogged into the woods he decided to stop and watch from a distance. His Exceptional eyes could see far, so there was little chance she would spot him. Pax and Maver had complained but when Luke had told them to go back to the City alone, they had decided to stick around.

When Luke saw the Exceptional Guards sneak up behind the girl and treat her roughly, it had lit a fire inside of him. He had never felt so angry over the treatment of an Ordinary before, and right then and there, he knew he had to do something about it. Pax and Maver had argued with him for a few minutes, claiming that they would get in trouble for being outside the City. But Luke's father was a powerful man, and he found that he could bend the rules more easily because of it.

Now he had claimed an Ordinary and was leading her through the entry tunnel that led into the City. He kept telling himself that he had done it because of the pressure from his parents, but deep down he had felt another need for claiming this girl. Ally, she had said her name was. He had felt drawn to her from the moment he laid eyes on her at the creek. With her dark features, bright green eyes, and the sheet of dark hair that blew behind her in the wind; her image was skillfully haunting.

But as they walked into the courtyard that served as the first checkpoint into the City, he was beginning to rethink the choice he had made. Ordinarys were given the opportunity to volunteer their way into the City, and this girl had not made that choice. He wasn't even sure why the Exceptional Guards had taken her in the first place. It wasn't a normal practice, and something about it made Luke wonder what the Guards had really had planned for her; if they were even planning on processing her into the City at all.

They passed through the courtyard and entered double doors that were built into a smaller version of the outer wall. As they stepped into the outskirts of the City, Luke took hold of Ally's arm again. She was busy gazing around them, taking in her new surroundings. Her head shot up at the sight of the large buildings that towered over the suburban homes.

"Luke." Corporal Byron, a solider he knew well, walked toward their group. He held a porta-comp in his hand, which meant the other

Guards had most likely sent him an e-comm about the situation. "Care to explain this to me?"

Byron motioned at Ally with his hand, talking as if she were not standing there.

"It was a simple misunderstanding. I met this girl at the boundary line and she told me that she had wanted to volunteer when the caravan last came through, but had missed her opportunity. Knowing it would please my father, I decided to step forward and claim her. I had to walk away for just a moment and the Guards pounced on her in my absence. We worked it out though."

Byron narrowed his eyes. "I would hope so."

He raised the porta-comp and slipped his finger along the touch screen. Ally would receive a temporary ID until the paperwork for her permanent position went through. Since they were going through this process backwards, things would be more complicated than usual.

Byron turned toward her. "Name?"

"Allona," she responded. "Allona of the family of Luella."

Luke had forgotten that Ordinarys did not take last names. They identified themselves with the name of their oldest surviving family member.

"Settlement?" Byron continued.

"Oakwood." She stood there with her hands clasped in front of her, her head held high. Her green eyes peered up at the Corporal, never lowering.

Byron punched more information into the porta-comp and pressed a button on the side. A white identification bracelet printed from the bottom and he took Ally's arm, securing it tightly around her slender wrist.

"Her permanent paper work should arrive in a week or two. Shall I have it sent to your house?" he inquired.

Luke nodded. "That sounds perfect. Good evening, sir."

He led Ally away from the entrance; Pax and Maver close on his heels. They walked several blocks, making sure they were far from the guards, before stopping.

"What were you thinking?" Pax hissed under his breath.

"I'm normally all for adventure, Luke, but this is a bit much, don't you think?" Maver added.

"I'll see you both tomorrow," he responded, not wanting to openly display his feelings to his friends, or Ally, at the moment.

His friends stood in place a minute longer before stomping off in the direction of their respective homes. He counted to ten in his head and then turned to face Ally, who was looking at something down the street.

"I'm not even sure what to say," he said slowly, watching her carefully.

She tore her eyes from the buildings and looked up at him. "How many are there?"

"Hmm?"

"Of those large buildings. They stretch so high up. There are too many trees in the settlement to view them from home, this is the first time I've seen them."

"Oh, I guess I've never thought about how many there are. A dozen or two maybe. Those are nothing. Apparently back before the virus, those buildings stretched almost one hundred stories high. Now the tallest building stops at twelve stories."

She looked upward once more. The buildings reflected the

bright orange sky, a result of the setting sun. It was the start of summer and the days were still lengthening, which meant the sun wouldn't disappear completely until well after dinner.

"Follow me." He realized he was still holding onto her arm and withdrew his hand, giving her some space.

She walked beside him quietly, showing no signs that she would attempt an escape. He led her out onto the main road, the one that would take them to his house the fastest. Most of the City citizens were inside for dinner, but a few still wandered the street. He watched as Ally observed them, turning her head sometimes to catch a second glimpse. Every now and then she would notice an Ordinary that walked through the street, carrying groceries or laundry bags, and a small smile filled her face.

Luke had only seen her smile once, and it was after she landed the jump across the boundary, when she thought no one but the other male Ordinary was watching. It had quickened the pace of his heart, and made him wonder what else it took to make her smile like that. It was genuine and kind, something many of the female Exceptionals in the City seemed to lack.

They passed the cramped town homes of the outer suburbs and turned into his neighborhood, one of the only areas with large homes that were spaced out. His parent's house was one of the first on the block. He led Ally up the walk and through the unlocked front door.

"Wow," Ally whispered as they stepped inside. "My whole house could fit in your foyer."

Luke felt uncomfortable by her comment. He had never thought much of his home before, since he hadn't any friends that lived in the cramped town homes. In fact, he had never given much thought to Ordinarys until a few weeks ago, and here he was bringing one home. What type of homes did they live in, in the settlement? Some of the Exceptionals he attended the Institute with went as far as to suggest Ordinarys lived in huts made of sticks and dried mud.

"Lukin!" His mother danced into the foyer, her voice chirping as she greeted him. "I'm so glad you are home. I was starting to worry. You weren't out getting into trouble again?"

Her long, silver hair was piled high on her head, held in place with a black headband. Her cheeks and lips were bright pink, and she had painted her eyelids a bright blue. She wore a bright yellow robe that dragged on the floor as she walked.

"No, mother," he responded.

"And who is this?" She took notice of Ally, who was still standing still by his side.

"This is Ally, mother. The Ordinary I have chosen."

His mother squealed, "Oh Lukin, your father will be so pleased. Did you visit the ORC this afternoon? Is that where you were? Why didn't you tell me? I would have gone with you. Although, you picked out such a beautiful girl on your own."

His mother reached her hand up to stroke Ally's face but he pushed it away. "Let's not scare her too much, Mother. Let me show her to her room and then we'll join the others for dinner."

His mother shrugged and danced back out of the room. She had always been eccentric and spacey, and he didn't need Ally's first impression of his family to be his mother in all her glory.

"This way." He started up the staircase that spiraled around the foyer. At the landing he led her down the hall to the right and stopped at the end. He pushed open one of the doors and stepped in.

"This will be your room while you are here. You'll be sharing with Sabine, whom I think you'll enjoy. She is about your age, and has been with our family for a long time. She runs the majority of the errands and does the laundry."

"It's huge," Ally said, walking toward one of the twin beds and running her fingers along the white comforter.

Luke didn't want to show her his room after her reaction to this. It was at the opposite end of the hall, and at least three times this size. He had his own bathroom, a TV, and a great view of the city. Ally's new room had two beds, a sofa, a reading corner, and a view of the backyard. She would share a hall bathroom with the other Ordinarys who lived here.

"I'll have Sabine bring you a few sets of clothes in the morning. She can also show you around while I'm at the Institute," He said, leaning against the doorframe.

Ally just nodded, still running her hand back and forth along the comforter. She took a seat and looked toward him, pushing her dark hair out of her eyes. "Institute?"

He opened his mouth to explain but just shook his head. "It isn't important. We should go down to dinner."

She nodded and stood, rubbing her hands on her pants. "Should I wash up?"

"You can wash up down there. Mazzi, the cook, will come looking for us if we don't show soon." He laughed slightly but stopped when Ally just stared at him, her face void of emotion.

By the time they got to the kitchen, his parents and the other Ordinarys were all gathered, waiting on dinner. Luke was surprised to see his father, since he spent most of his nights at the office. He

33

wondered if he would be required to eat in the dining room with his parents, or if he could stay and dine in the kitchen with Ally.

"Father," he said, waiting.

His father looked up at him, looking very annoyed that he had been interrupted. "Lukin."

"I would like you to meet Ally."

His father noticed Ally for the first time now, studying her carefully.

"Ally, this is my father," Luke announced.

"Mr. Mathias," His father corrected.

"I know who you are, sir." Ally stepped forward. "You're Aden. The city leader."

His father smirked and put his porta-comp into the pocket of his suit coat. "Good. Then you'll truly understand your place in this house. Now if you'll excuse me, I think I'll be dining in my bedroom this evening."

Luke watched his father leave the room with his plate of food, and waited until he heard him close his office door before he turned to Ally. "Sorry about that, he isn't always the most pleasant person to be around. Especially after a long day at the office."

Luke's mother seemed oblivious to everything that had just happened. She took her plate of food and left the kitchen, wandering down the first floor hall.

Ally shrugged. "It isn't anything I haven't seen from the Exceptional Guards outside the City. I'm just glad he didn't push me down."

Her tone told him that she was joking, but her words still bothered him. He had seen first hand a Guard pushing her down in the

34

woods, and he wondered if it was a regular occurrence in the settlements. He shook his head, turning toward the kitchen.

"This is Mazzi, our cook and my second mother." He motioned to Mazzi, a plump Ordinary who always dressed with an eccentric style that could compete with his mother's.

Ally waved at Mazzi and turned to the others.

"This is Sabine, your roommate, and Asher and Flint. They are all Ordinarys that work in the house, so you'll get to know them very well over the next several weeks."

He never took his eyes off her, watching her expression carefully. Her smile seemed to falter when he mentioned a length of time that she would be here, but it only lasted a second.

"Hi, I'm Ally," she said, looking them over.

They seemed to be doing the same, attempting to figure out her place in the house. Since Ally hadn't come from the ORC, she didn't know as much as any other Ordinary would have coming into an Exceptional home. Because of this, he would need to warn the others not to mention anything to her. He wanted to tell Ally about her purpose here on his own, but he didn't think it would be best to give her that information right from the start. She needed some time to acclimate to the household, and hopefully, find a place in his family.

Chapter Four

The following morning, Ally had almost forgotten where she had fallen asleep. The night before had been a blur, especially after Aden had stalked out of the room. Luke had introduced her to the other workers in the house before they all sat down for dinner. His presence seemed to make the three younger Ordinarys somber, and they ended up eating the majority of the meal in silence. Luke's father called him into his office toward the end of the meal and he excused himself quickly. Asher and Flint, the two boys, shoveled their food down fast and disappeared to work on their final chores. Sabine had gone to finish some laundry, which left Ally in the kitchen with just Mazzi. When she had finished dinner, Ally went up to their room on her own and settled into bed, falling asleep quickly.

When she woke up, the events of the previous day still floated through her mind like a fog. She'd been so overwhelmed by the sight of the City, Luke, and her new home, that she hadn't processed many emotions last night. Luke had tried to be kind to her, had even tried to make her laugh, but she had felt nothing. Hadn't she thought about volunteering to come here just a few months back? She decided that there would have been more preparation involved. She would have been ready to enter the City and take on her new job. But yesterday she had fully expected to be back in the settlement with her family. Today was Tuesday, a workday, and she probably would have been up and getting ready for a long day of gathering.

She battled her way out of the overly plush blanket on the bed and swung her feet over the edge. She noticed a fresh pair of clothes sitting on the dresser near the door. Had Sabine put those there or someone else? She looked down at her own clothes. They were ratty and dirty, and she was sure they smelled worse than anything else in this house ever had. She grabbed the pile of clean clothes, which she realized were the same muted gray color she had seen on Luke yesterday, and found her way down the hall and into the shared bathroom.

Back at the settlement most bathroom needs were taken care of outside since the houses didn't have running water. They did have electricity though, which was provided by the City. It was a foreign motion for her to grab on to the handle of the faucet and turn it on. The water even came out warm, which didn't happen at home unless it was boiled over a fire. She splashed some on her face, letting it drip down her cheeks and onto her worn shirt.

"You're up!" The voice startled Ally, and she turned around with her arms raised protectively.

Sabine stood in the doorway, a large grin on her face. She was dressed in the same gray clothes that Ally had taken from the dresser, and her long, red hair was pulled back into a braid. Ally relaxed almost immediately, happy to see a friendly face.

"I'm supposed to show you how the shower works, and where your supply of clothes will be held," Sabine said, stepping into the bathroom.

She walked over to the shower in the corner and opened the glass door. Ally had a shower in the bathroom she shared with her mother, but it was nonfunctional so they used it to store extra belongings.

"You grab this handle and turn it to the left. Try to match this arrow up with the middle of the red area, which seems to be a good shower temperature in my opinion. When you are finished you just turn it all the way to the right." She stepped away from the shower and flashed Ally another smile. "The white bottle there is a cleanser for your hair, and there is a fresh bar of soap in the corner. Got it?"

Ally just nodded, thinking it sounded simple enough.

"Good. Your clothes are kept in the dresser where you found today's pair. You'll have seven sets of clothes since laundry goes out to be done once a week. Mr. Mathias might eventually give you a chore list, but I'm not sure when, or if he even will."

"Aden?"

"Luke," Sabine said slowly.

"Oh, so I should call him Mr. Mathias as well?"

Sabine giggled. "That or Mr. Lukin. You'll catch on quick. Soon it will be second nature to call him something so formal."

Sabine rambled on about Ordinary meal times and rules for behavior. According to Sabine, they were only allowed to leave the property on work order, but they could go into the backyard at any time. They were also never to address the housemasters unless spoken to first. Ally had already broken that rule yesterday when she addressed Aden, and all the times she had spoken to Luke the day before. Sabine finally slipped from the bathroom and left Ally in peace.

She slipped out of her clothes and put them in a pile by the door. She would need to throw those into the trash once she was ready to go downstairs. She stepped into the shower and walked through what Sabine had shown her. Ally heard the pipes creak as water sprinkled from the showerhead up above. Cold water fell over her body, but she didn't mind. She was used to taking cold baths, and in a matter of seconds, the water heated up to a comfortable level.

She grabbed the bottle that Sabine had said was hair cleanser. Back in the settlement they rinsed their hair with water from the creek, nothing additional. She twisted the cap off the bottle and tipped it toward her free hand. More than she thought she might be required to use poured out into her hand, but she worked it all into her long hair anyway. The substance changed as she worked it in deeper, leaving Ally's hands covered in white foam. She rinsed the foam from her hair and then used the bar of soap, something she at least recognized from home.

Ten minutes later she was clean, dry, and dressed in her new clothes. The clothes were similar to the ones she had previously owned, except the material felt softer and more durable. She used her fingers to brush her hair out since she couldn't find a comb, and let it hang loose behind her. When she stepped out into the hall, Sabine was waiting for her.

"Feel better?" she asked.

Ally nodded and followed Sabine down the stairs and into the kitchen.

Asher and Flint were already standing by the counter, occupying the same space Aden stood in last night. Ally had dreamt of his dangerous eyes last night, not being able to shake the fear of him quite yet. She had tried to appear fearless when she spoke to him, but his appearance and mannerisms had been intimidating.

A few minutes later, Mazzi served them each a plate of eggs, toast, and what looked like some sort of meat. They all sat down at the table together and Ally dug into her breakfast. She hadn't eaten much

39

dinner last night and as the smell of eggs reached her nose, her stomach rumbled in protest.

The Ordinary that Ally thought she remembered as Asher leaned toward her. "Oakwood settlement?"

She paused mid bite and nodded. "How did you know?"

The male next to him rolled his eyes. "Asher here has a knack for guessing which settlement an Ordinary originated from."

"I'm always right, Flint."

"Ninety-five percent of the time…"

Ally smiled and pulled up the sleeve of her shirt, showing them the marking on her wrist.

"I've only see a handful of those before," Sabine said as she leaned in for a closer look. "Does it hurt when they do that?"

"Oh yeah, a ton." Ally ran her finger over the bumpy scar. "But they give you a special ointment afterward that dulls the pain. Don't you all have one?"

"We aren't from the settlements," Asher said. "We were all born and raised in the city."

Ally knew her mouth was hanging open but she didn't care at the moment. "Born in the City? I didn't know that happened."

Asher and Flint both laughed out loud and Sabine shot her a confused look. "What did you think happened to all the Ordinarys? That we worked our lives away and died with out marrying, or having children, or any of that?" Sabine said.

Ally pursed her lips. "I guess I hadn't given it much thought before now."

Their conversation was interrupted as Mrs. Mathias bounced into the room, barking orders at Mazzi. She tapped her long fingernails

40

on the shiny black counter top while the cook ran around trying to prepare her breakfast.

"Good morning, Ally," she said, her bright pink lips forming a smile. "I see you've met the others. I hope they are helping you make a smooth transition into our home."

"Yes, very much so." Ally responded as politely as she could, realizing that since she had been spoken to first, she could speak back.

"Good good!" Mrs. Mathias spurted out, grabbing the plate that Mazzi had just laid on the counter. "Lots to do today."

She disappeared from the room just as quickly as she had come, leaving them all staring after her.

"She likes you," Asher said when they heard Mrs. Mathias slam a door in the distance. "Consider yourself lucky."

"That's because Mr. Lukin has claimed her," Sabine giggled.

Ally perked up. "Oh, I meant to ask you about that. What exactly does it mean when you say he *claimed* me?"

The table fell into an awkward silence. Even the kitchen grew quiet, when just a moment ago it had been filled with the sounds of Mazzi cleaning the dishes. Flint suddenly became very interested in his food and Asher cleared his throat.

"Let me take you on a tour," Sabine avoided Ally's question, trying to diffuse the tension in the room. "We don't want you getting lost."

Ally thought about bringing the conversation back to her question, but decided there was time for that later. Right now, a tour of Luke's home sounded somewhat interesting.

First she learned that the darkened hallway on the first floor was completely off limits to Ordinarys. She was pretty sure it was the same hall that Mrs. Mathias had disappeared down earlier. There was a sitting room on the first floor that held hundreds of books; a room Sabine had called a library. Back at the settlement, all of the remaining books were kept in glass cases. A few times a year one of the adults would read one out loud to them all, but no one else was allowed to touch the book.

Sabine informed Ally that the black object in the foyer was a piano and that it made music when played correctly. When she asked if anyone in the home could play it she just smiled and pulled Ally into the next room, quickly becoming an expert at avoiding questions. There was a large dining room toward the front of the house where Aden sometimes hosted parties. Most of the second floor was devoted to guest rooms, except for two rooms at the end. Asher and Flint occupied one, and Sabine occupied the other. Luke's room was at the opposite end of the hall, and also off limits unless a work order said to enter.

Sabine paused at the railing that overlooked the foyer. "Ally, what do you know about your purpose here?"

"Nothing. One moment I was playing a seemingly innocent game in the woods, and the next I was being brought in by the Exceptional Guards," Ally responded.

"You mean you didn't volunteer?"

Ally shook her head. "Luke found me out in the woods and rescued me, if you could call it that. That was just yesterday afternoon."

"You didn't even come from the ORC?"

"What's the ORC?" Ally had heard Mrs. Mathias mention it last night.

"Sabine!" a male voice yelled from the foyer, either Asher or Flint. "We need to go!"

"We'll talk later," Sabine said as she squeezed Ally's arm. "Flint

42

and I need to run errands."

Sabine skipped down the stairs, her red braid bouncing against her back as she went. As Ally turned, she caught a glimpse of Asher standing in the doorway to his room.

"You have no idea what you are in for." He smirked and shut his bedroom door, leaving Ally to digest his words alone.

She thought about stomping up to his door and confronting him, but she still couldn't muster up the old Ally from within. Where was the daring and wild Ally that was always up for an adventure? Where was the Ally that had no problem standing up for herself or others? She was beginning to worry that she was in some sort of shock. She had always said that if she volunteered, she wouldn't let the City take her personality. She would be living in a different place, with a different purpose, but she could still be herself. Now here she was, cowering under the roof of an Exceptional home on her very first day.

She moved down the stairs quickly, entering the library. She had never seen so many books, but even if she wanted to read them, it would do her no good. They didn't learn to read in the settlement unless it was decided that it was a crucial part of their future work assignment. As a food gatherer, she wasn't even given the opportunity to learn to write.

Ally ran her fingers over the old books, loving the way the worn covers felt under her fingers. She pulled a book out every now and then, admiring the cover and imagining what story the picture might represent. Her best friend, Willow, had been training to be a town medic, and therefore had been taught to read. She wished Willow were here right now, telling her what all the words in these books said. She imagined most of them were quite interesting.

"That one is about forbidden love."

Ally jumped. She turned to find Mrs. Mathias standing behind her, looking over her shoulder at the book. She had been so enamored with the cover image that she hadn't even heard Luke's mother enter the room.

"Forbidden love?" she asked.

Mrs. Mathias smiled. "It is a common theme in love stories, but this one was quite famous in its time. It is about two lovers from feuding families. They fall in love despite their differences, and bring much grief to those around them. In the end, their love for each other is their demise."

Ally gave the book one last look and slipped it back onto the shelf. "That sounds horrible."

Mrs. Mathias let out a loud, cackling laugh. It reminded Ally of the cawing crows in the woods back home. "But still, it is a very romantic story, don't you think?"

"How?" Ally raised her eyebrow.

"Their love knew no bounds. It was strong enough to bring them together even though they knew their parents would never allow it. They chose to follow their hearts, rather than the wills of others, all for love. It affirms to us that love is a powerful thing."

Ally considered her words. "Their love wasn't strong enough to conquer their deaths."

"Is it ever?" Mrs. Mathias said with a smile. With that she hopped out of the room, leaving Ally to herself.

Ally wondered if the other books contained stories that were just as upsetting. She couldn't imagine a love that forced her death in the end, but then again, she had never been in love. She had never given it much thought before, and chose not to give it anymore thought that morning. She slipped out of the library and left the stacks of mysterious stories behind.

Chapter Five

Sabine and Flint didn't return until later that afternoon. Ally and Asher had eaten lunch together but shared no conversation during their time at the table, which was just fine with Ally considering his earlier comment. He had eaten quickly, mumbling something about shredding documents and alphabetizing books. Ally was ready to pounce on Sabine the moment she saw her appear around the corner. She wanted—

no needed— to know more. Their parting words had been on her mind all day and she couldn't stand the anticipation much longer.

As luck would have it, Luke stormed through the door at the same time and grabbed Ally's arm, dragging her up the stairs and into his bedroom. She had to run to keep up with him since his Exceptional strength allowed him to move quickly with out much effort. His room was huge, much larger than the bedroom she shared with Sabine. The bed was twice the size as well, and covered in a fluffy, white comforter similar to the one on the bed in her room. All her observations were lost the moment her eyes locked on the large, black object that hung on the wall directly opposite of the bed. It had a rectangular shape to it, and almost reminded her of the computer the City had given Po back in the settlement. The one he used to communicate with the Exceptionals when necessary.

Lukin dropped a stack of books on the floor and turned to face her. "What did they tell you?"

She tore her eyes from the strange box and stared at him.

"Who?"

She wasn't sure exactly what he was alluding to, but his face showed a mixture of anger and nervousness.

"The Ordinarys. Sabine, Asher, and Flint."

Ally wondered if Luke was driven to this line of questioning by whatever Sabine had been trying to tell her earlier. "We didn't talk much today. Sabine and Flint were on errands for the majority of it, and Asher was doing chores. I spent a good portion of my time in the library looking at book covers. I even had a conversation with your mother. Honestly, that was the extent of my day."

"My mother talked to you?" The corner of his mouth pulled up into a smile. "And you haven't run screaming from the house?"

Ally allowed herself to laugh. "It wasn't the most conventional conversation I've ever had, but it was informative."

Lukin seemed to mull that over, his violet eyes narrowing as they studied her. They were so bright they almost glowed, and Ally searched for a reason to look away.

"What is that?" She pointed back to the contraption hanging on the wall.

He followed her finger and let out a small laugh. "That? That's a TV. We use it to play movies. Before the virus it played shows and programs from around the world, but the ability to do so was lost long ago."

"Movies?" All of these words were foreign to her, and she suddenly wished she had paid more attention to the stories her grandfather used to tell. He would tell her and Stosh that they needed to listen close, because if no one carried the stories on, soon the old world would be completely forgotten. But Ally didn't see the problem in that; the old world would never be coming back.

"I'll show you," he said.

She followed him over to the TV and sat on the sofa while he looked through a cabinet nearby. He pulled a small box from within and opened it, pulling out a thin, circular object. Several minutes later, Lukin had the movie playing on the TV. It hadn't taken long, and Ally was sure she could repeat the steps if she tried hard enough.

Pictures came to life on the screen. The people in them moved, talked, shouted, and even kissed at times. The movie they were watching seemed to be some sort of romance, with a war thrown in the middle. Wars were a thing of the past, something she did actually recall from her grandfather's stories. He had said that her great grandfather had fought in one of the country's more extensive wars, and had been in the military when the SS-16 virus was created.

"It's amazing, Lukin... I mean, Mr. Lukin," she commented, watching the movie in awe.

"Yeah, I guess. And please, call me Luke," he said as he cocked his head at her, something she noticed out of the corner of her eye.

"But Sabine..."

"Forget what she said. I give you permission to call me by my first name, and by that I mean you can call me *Luke*. Only my parents call me Lukin anymore."

With that, he turned back to the movie and leaned back into the couch. They watched the remainder of it in silence, which gave Ally a chance to take it all in.

48

"Some of these things seem so unreal. Bombs that could blow up whole towns, planes that people flew in, the clothes they wore, the animals they kept in their homes; all of it," Ally said as the movie came to a close.

"I've seen these movies several times, and have had time to grow used to the idea of old world objects, but sometimes I still have trouble believing such things existed. The City use to be full of cars and other forms of transportation, but now we walk wherever we go. Some Exceptionals have bikes, which I can show you later, but learning to ride them is a pain," Luke responded.

The TV screen turned black. White scribbles scrolled up the screen and soft music played in the background. Luke stood and turned the TV off, returning the movie to its case.

"Do you want to leave the house for a bit? We can go for a walk and I can show you more of the City," he asked.

Ally jumped up. "Yes."

She hadn't realized how much she was already missing the outdoors. She practically lived outside her home in the settlement when she wasn't eating or sleeping, and it had been almost a full day since she had breathed fresh air in the City. She ran to the bathroom to pull her hair back and then met Luke in the foyer, a well-missed feeling of excitement overcoming her. Perhaps she wasn't in shock after all.

ALLY DECIDED that the City looked more magnificent in the daylight. There had barely been any daylight left when she had arrived the night before. The buildings were completely visible in the cloudless sky, and the streets were scattered with Exceptionals and Ordinarys out for the afternoon. Ally noticed that all of the Ordinarys were wearing the

49

same grey clothes that she wore, while the Exceptionals' clothes were stark white, just like the large comforter that covered Ally's bed. Now that she thought about it, Luke's house was filled with white rugs, walls, and other white objects of all sorts.

"Where are all these Exceptionals going?" Ally asked Luke. There were too many of them for them to all be from his living area.

"They are coming home from City Center, either from work or errands. This is the most direct route," he responded, weaving through a group of chatty female Exceptionals.

Ally watched as another group of Exceptionals passed by. She was awestruck by how similar they looked to the friends and family she grew up with back in the settlement. If she wasn't able to see their violet eyes, and the boys with the shaved heads, she might have mistaken them for Ordinarys. Every now and then they would pass a Guard on patrol and Ally's insides would turn. These were the Exceptionals she had grown to fear.

"This way." Luke took hold of her hand and pulled her in the opposite direction the crowd was moving.

They finally burst out onto a side street that was less crowded, but he didn't let go of her hand. The houses were growing smaller and closer together, many having no space between them at all. Other buildings were scattered throughout the houses, with signs hanging outside that Ally couldn't read. One building had a stand of fruit sitting outside the door and she wondered if they were being sold to the Exceptionals and Ordinarys in the City.

After another half mile of weaving through the streets, they came upon an open area filled with benches and tables. A few small trees grew in the grassy area in the middle, but Ally was immediately taken with the large tree directly in the middle.

"What is it?" Luke came up beside her.

Ally pulled back her sleeve and held out her arm. "It's an Oak tree, almost identical to my marking."

"Whoa," he said, running his finger over her mark.

She shivered and pulled her arm back, confused by the feeling that ran through her when Luke had touched her. She cleared her throat, trying to disguise her uncertainty.

"The branches even grow in similar directions." Ally pointed out. She didn't mention that she was also thinking about how quickly she could climb the tree. Partially because it was off topic, but mainly because he might think her insane for even considering it.

If he had any idea that she was undergoing some strange inner battle, he didn't let on. Rather, he took a seat on one of the benches beneath the tree. She did the same, sliding to the opposite end of the bench and clasping her hands together in her lap.

"You must have a lot of questions." Luke peered over at her.

Ally was still having trouble figuring him out. His confidence and arrogance when they first met had scared her at first, but had also given her a fierce attraction toward him. But without his friends or parents around, he was kind and gentle. He seemed interested in helping her learn about the City, and making her feel comfortable in his home. There was something attractive about this Luke as well. Ally had to believe that maybe she just found him appealing as a whole, no matter what state his personality happened to be in. He was fairly handsome.

"Yes," she answered quickly. Her pause in conversation had

evoked a reaction from him, and he had begun to slide toward her on the bench.

Ally had been so anxious for answers all day, and now she felt speechless when she was finally getting her chance. Her first instinct was to ask a question that would help her understand what Sabine had been about to tell her earlier, but she feared Luke wouldn't answer. Plus, if he knew Sabine was talking about it, he might order her not to give Ally further information.

She turned to face him. "The only Exceptionals I have ever known are the Guards, so you can understand why I might be a little amazed at this whole other world that exists inside the City. Even though I know that not every Exceptional is a Guard, it was hard to picture everyone within the walls in any other way. What was growing up here like?"

Luke's smile faded slightly at her question. "In turn, we aren't told much about Ordinarys and their lives outside of the City. We only know what... what we use them for. Ordinarys aren't spoken of much during every day activities, unless one is needed for a chore or task."

He seemed to be thinking carefully about his word choices. "You've met my father, and you know who he is, so you should know that my upbringing was much different than that of the other Exceptionals. I'm not really a great example of an average Exceptional in the City. We all start attending the Institute young so we can be assessed for our future potential. When I wasn't in lessons, I was with my best friends, Pax and Maver, whom you have met. We mainly would watch movies or go to the Warehouse in City Center."

Ally raised her hand to stop him. She had seen movies in action but hadn't heard him mention the place before. "Warehouse?"

Luke leaned back, resting his arms on the back of the bench. His fingers came close to touching Ally's shoulder. "The Warehouse is a building where younger Exceptionals gather to play games and be together. Once an Exceptional turns eighteen, he or she is no longer allowed to go. We are required to focus on our higher level classes at that point."

"And how old are you?" The thought popped into Ally's head.

"I'll be eighteen in a little over a month."

Ally smiled. "I am eighteen today."

Luke perked up. "Really? Why didn't you say anything?"

"Were you planning on making me a cake?" She raised her eyebrow and he smiled.

Ally changed the subject. "So this Institute, what are you taking these classes for?"

Luke's jaw tightened. "I already mentioned the assessments we receive when we are younger. Those results are combined with the scores you receive in your lessons over the next several years. Once you enter higher education you are put on a career path. It is more training than learning. For instance, Pax is being groomed to be a Guard. This means that his day is filled with lessons on shooting guns and disabling unruly civilians, or something similar."

Ally gasped. "A Guard? But he doesn't even fit the description!"

She watched as Luke's face took on a grim appearance. "That doesn't mean that he won't once he has completed all of his training."

Ally felt sick. "And you? What are you being trained for?"

"To work in leadership, like my father."

She could tell he wasn't happy with the path he had been given. She took her gaze off his face and stared at the ground in front of her for a while. Despite being an Exceptional and growing up with more luxuries than Ally could have ever hoped to enjoy, in a way, Luke was a lot like her. He had still been a kid, he had still had friends, and he had still been forced to do things he didn't want to do.

"Ally, were you ever told stories about the days during the spread of the virus?" He leaned forward, resting his elbows on his knees.

"My grandfather told me bits and pieces, but the elders were discouraged from talking too much about the old world. It has been long enough that many of the memories and stories have died off," Ally responded.

He continued. "Somehow someone captured small pieces of that time on film and preserved it for the future to see. They show us the videos when we first get to the Institute so that we can see just what we came from. It was chaos. Ninety percent of the world's population was infected, and only a small portion of those infected survived. They became what I am now, what we all call Exceptionals. They had to deal with not only the death of their friends and family and the possible destruction of their world, but with their newfound powers. Most experienced extra strength, outstanding hearing, and sight that rivaled that of any other creature on Earth. Some of the Exceptionals even experienced extra powers. One man found himself capable of creating fire in the palms of his hands, while another could create ice that could put that flame out. One man could move objects with his mind, while another could transport himself a few feet at a time."

"That doesn't seem possible." Ally had heard rumors of Exceptional Guards with abnormal powers, more abnormal than what they already were. She had never seen it for herself though.

"It shouldn't be. But neither should our super strength, hearing, or eyesight. Exceptionals are even able to process information faster than an Ordinary. I can read a whole book in an hour and remember everything."

Ally didn't take his statement as bragging, he didn't seem proud of it.

"What happened to those Exceptionals, the ones with the extra powers?"

Luke looked up at the tree branch hanging just over their heads. "They still exist. In fact, ninety-nine percent of Exceptionals have extra abilities, but most do not flaunt them openly. Many of these abilities are minor, like spouting a weak stream of water from the finger tips."

That sounded pretty remarkable to Ally, but she let him continue.

"My father is one of those Exceptionals with abilities that makes him rise above the others. It is one of the reasons he is in the position he is in now. But my father likes power, and he'll do anything to gather others with just as much power. To either make them friends or eliminate them."

Ally shivered at the thought. "What about you? Do you have extra abilities?"

"Nothing as great as my father's abilities, and I'm glad. I don't want to be power hungry like him, and I don't want to be one of his tools," he said as he stood and offered her his hand. "We should get back. Mazzi will be serving dinner soon."

The sky had started to take on a golden twinge, signaling that the sun was starting to make its decent into the horizon. They walked back to his house in silence, his hand still grasping hers. There were fewer Exceptionals and Ordinarys on the street than before, and when they stepped into his house they were greeted with silence.

"I have to eat dinner with my father and mother tonight. Once a month my mother makes sure we are both under the same roof, and that all three of us eat in the same room." He rolled his eyes. "I figure I might as well humor her. I'm going to go wash up, but you should head to the kitchen to eat with the others."

Ally nodded and stepped away from him, hoping that she would find Sabine in the kitchen. She still wanted to hear more about Luke and his family from her. She had been afraid to ask Luke any more personal questions when they had been sitting on the bench, and once he had begun to talk about his father, his mood had soured considerably.

Sabine, Asher, and Flint were all standing by the counter when she entered the room. Mazzi was busy cooking, which she always seemed to be doing, and a sweet scent filled the air.

"It smells delicious in here," Ally commented as she joined them.

"Where have you been?" Sabine put a hand on her hip and tried to look stern. It was a face her mother used a lot when she and Stosh were younger.

"On a walk with Luke." She didn't add anything further.

Sabine's frown turned into a smile, Flint looked bored, and Asher looked somewhat amused. She had a feeling it would take a while to figure out the rhythm between these three but she was willing to try. She might spend the rest of her life in this house with them, and she wanted her friendships to count. Otherwise, it would be a long, lonely life.

Mazzi served them up four plates of glazed ham, cooked carrots, and a large helping of mashed potatoes. These were foods that Ally only had a few times a year, and here it seemed that they were being fed this well each day.

"Is the food always this good?" Ally said as they sat down.

"Always." Asher popped a carrot into his mouth. "The Exceptionals believe in treating the Ordinarys inside the City a little bit better than the ones outside. We aren't much use to them starved and miserable."

Ally shot him a dirty look, but in a way he was right. They were always fed back in the settlement, but the food was nothing compared to what she was eating for dinner. Their meat was always tough and fatty, and their carrots didn't taste this good. She realized that Mazzi had put some sort of sauce on them as well, and in the settlement their food didn't come with any extras.

"I finished my work list before dinner, so I think I'm going to turn in early. Mrs. Mathias had Flint and I running all over the City today," Sabine said between bites of ham.

Ally nodded. "I wouldn't mind turning in early, either. It's been a long day."

Her day had started off slow, but after her talk with Luke she felt as though she had been in the City for days. There were so many new things to remember, new people to meet, and emotions to work through. She fell into bed later that night, her mind was racing with all of the information she had received today. Hadn't she always dreamt of coming to the City? Her family had held her back, and she had been willing to stay in the settlement, but fate had intervened. She wanted to find a way to enjoy her time in the Mathias household, but a small part of her felt that there was something bigger behind her being here. That she didn't quite know everything about her necessity to Luke, and why of all the Ordinarys, he had chosen her.

Chapter Six

As he lay in bed that same night, Luke thought about how well Ally was starting to fit into his life already. He had expected she would be nervous and afraid, and maybe even reserved at first. The first night had been questionable, but then she warmed right up, willing to spend time with him and be around him without being disgusted. He would be disgusted with himself if the situation were reversed, but he hadn't had a chance to tell her the truth yet, to really explain her purpose here. He had been fearful that Sabine or one of the other Ordinarys might break the news, but he had broken down and told them not to. He didn't give out many orders when it came to their house workers, but he decided to make an exception for this.

He hadn't believed it possible to become so captivated with a girl in such a short time. He had attended the Institute with hundreds of them, and many of them had found interest in him, but he knew it was most likely because of who his father was, and of who he might become one day. If he hadn't known Pax and Maver since before he could walk, he might be tempted to forgo normal friendships as well. There was no one else he could trust.

The night before, when he had been called from dinner, his father had asked him some questions about the new "Ordinary" in their house. Had he talked to her about the contract? Had he made a decision on the specifics? How quickly would he progress to the desired result? Luke had tried to give his father answers, but he couldn't think of much to say. He had finally excused himself and shut himself in his room, watching a few romance movies he had never bothered to pull off the shelf before. These feelings were new to him, and he hoped he could gain some wisdom from the old world.

Luke had felt better after his afternoon with Ally, but as he fell asleep that evening, he knew there were many things he still needed to tell her. Hopefully he would find the time to talk to her in the morning and explain more.

LUKE KNOCKED on Ally's door just before breakfast. When she opened it, her dark hair was freshly washed and hanging in wet tendrils down her back and shoulders. She was wearing the standard muted gray outfit that Ordinarys wore, and had already slipped into the black work shoes each Ordinary was provided.

"I thought we could spend some more time together today. I don't have any lessons at the Institute, and no plans with Pax or Maver."

Ally stepped into the hallway and closed the bedroom door behind her. "Oh, well, sure. I thought maybe you were coming to give me my work list."

He laughed. "Did you *want* a work list?"

She shrugged. "It would make me feel more useful. I don't want to sit around the house while the others run around doing work."

He hadn't thought about it that way, but he also didn't like the idea of giving her chores to do. He didn't want Ally to think he owned her, even if, in a sense, he did. If he were ever to question the system that separated the Exceptionals from the Ordinarys, it would be now.

"So, time together?"

She smiled. "Sure."

They walked down the stairs and through the kitchen, passing through the glass double doors that led to the backyard. Luke's mother used to spend hours outside during the warm weather, tending to the garden and keeping the area well maintained. Now it was Asher's job to take care of the backyard, but it didn't look as grand. A brick patio stretched out from the back of the house, covering a third of the backyard. The rest of the yard was a sprawling garden, with stone paths that swirled and looped around, sometimes meeting each other at a crossroads. There was also a fountain in the back corner, one that Luke had played in as a child.

"It's beautiful." Ally approached a large pot with roses growing in it. "We only have wild flowers back in the settlement, and our gardens are strictly for growing food. Did your mother do all of this?"

Luke nodded. "She used to spend most of her time out here, but recently she has been locked up in her office."

"And why is that?" Ally stepped away from the roses and back toward him.

"I have no idea," he answered honestly.

She turned and headed toward the end of the patio, twirling around as she stepped onto one of the dirt paths. "You wanted to talk?"

He followed behind her, watching as she spun and skipped through the garden. Luke could tell she was more alive outside, as if the fresh air and smell of flowers breathed life into her. She stopped when they got to the fountain and sat down on a bench directly across from it. He took a seat next to her and studied her for a moment.

"What?" she asked, tilting her head to the side.

"Nothing. I've just never met anyone quite like you," he said.

"Is that a bad thing?"

He shook his head quickly. "No, not at all. All the Exceptionals in the City, and even Ordinarys, always seem to be in a rush. They always seem stressed, worried, and set on moving forward toward the next step in life. You seem so free, willing to pause and enjoy the moment."

Ally laughed, her head tilting up toward the sky as she did. "I never thought I would find an Exceptional envious of my life." She paused, her gaze meeting his again. "I almost volunteered to come to the City during the last gathering."

"Really? Why?" he asked.

She shrugged. "I never felt as though there was a future for me in the settlement. I liked the City because it was an unknown. Others volunteered, and it must be great if they never returned after their five-year contract is up. Did you know that not one Ordinary has come back to our settlement since they started gathering volunteers?"

Luke tried to keep his expression steady. "That's interesting. I never realized the City was such a big deal to those on the outside, but maybe it is because I grew up here. What was your settlement like?"

"You would laugh if you saw it after having lived here your whole life. The homes are much smaller than yours, and we live with one to two other families. The settlements used to be neighborhoods with multiple homes but some have crumpled to the ground. Because of this the placement of the homes is very sporadic, and they aren't well maintained. We receive electricity from the City, but no running water. My brother and I spent most of our childhood in the woods, climbing trees and playing games. That is something I really miss from the settlement. Trees."

Her cheeks turned a light pink.

"I shouldn't talk about it so negatively though. It really is a great place to be. I loved the freedom I had, being able to escape into the woods if I needed to get away. The Ordinarys are great as well. We were like one big family, each of us bringing our talents and interests together to work and live as one."

He could tell she was battling inwardly with which place was the right one for her, The City or her settlement.

"What would you be doing today if you were still in the settlement?" he asked.

She bit her lower lip while she thought. "Hmm. It would be a workday, so I would be out in the woods, either gathering food or hunting. We are assigned our jobs at fourteen, and then trained for one or two years before really getting involved. My brother is a woodcutter, while my mother is a seamstress."

"You've mentioned your brother before. Is that the boy I saw in the woods with you?" Luke thought back to the day he met Ally. It had been just two afternoons prior to this one.

She nodded. "Stosh. He is my twin brother; and my best friend."

"And your father?" Luke had noticed she omitted him from their conversation.

"I don't know who he is, and he doesn't know who I am either. My mother said he was gone before she knew she was pregnant with my brother and me"

"That doesn't seem fair."

"It is what it is."

"But doesn't it make you mad?" Luke leaned toward her.

"Should it?" she responded.

"I think so. It is okay to be angry and upset over something, even if you cannot change the outcome. They are normal human emotions, and you should allow yourself to feel them."

He was alluding to the fact that she could show some emotion in reaction to the events of the past couple of days, but he couldn't find the words to say it outright.

Ally watched him for a minute, her jaw line tightening. "Do you have any brothers or sisters?"

He shook his head. "No. When my mother gave birth to a son my father said there was no need for other children."

"He sounds lovely", she laughed.

"Look, Ally, there are some things I need to tell you…" Luke rubbed his clammy hands on his pants. He had stalled long enough, and now he needed to come clean.

She rested her chin in her hands, watching him.

"In the woods, when I claimed you from the Guards, I wasn't doing it to prove a point to them or just to save your life." He started, taking a different direction than he had planned. "I was truly interested in you from the moment I saw you. I want to get to know you better, if you'll give me a chance."

Ally seemed surprised at his words, her green eyes growing wide. She turned and stared at the fountain, bouncing her foot on the ground. She finally opened her mouth to speak, but another voice called out in the garden.

"Luke! Hey, Luke."

"Pax," he cursed under his breath.

"There you are." Pax ran into the garden and grinned when he saw Luke and Ally sitting on the bench. Luke hadn't realized it before, but they were sitting fairly close to each other. He moved over a few inches and turned toward his best friend. A moment later Maver slid up beside him.

"Luke," Maver started. "You need to come with us, now."

"Why?" He stood and stepped toward his friends. "I'm kind of busy here."

Pax laughed. "We can see that."

"Watch it," Luke snapped. "What is so important?"

Maver practically jumped beside them, his expression brimming with excitement. "Tighe has *challenged* you."

"What?" Luke let out a frustrated groan. "Today? I'm not even at the Warehouse, isn't this against the rules?"

Maver smirked. "He didn't do it officially. He told us to come get you, making sure to add that a refusal would be cowardly. We told him that you would come, and you would destroy him... again."

Pax slapped Luke on the shoulder. "Looks like any business you had with the Ordinary today is off. You have a fight to win."

Luke looked back at Ally, who was watching their interaction with curiosity. He didn't want to leave her, especially after she had started to open up to him, but he couldn't risk his friends seeing him have a weak moment. He hoped that what he said before Pax arrived had left some sort of good impression on her, and that she would start to trust him. Without a word he turned his back to her and followed his friends out of the garden.

Chapter Seven

When Luke left Ally in the garden, she had spent almost an hour wandering the paths, wearing a nice pattern into the already packed down stones. Luke's words settled into her mind. He was interested in *her*? Back in the settlement, dating had never been something she considered. A few of the boys her age had seemed interested, but she didn't want to be tied down to any relationship. Her mother's previous relationship had done more harm than good, and Ally wasn't sure she wanted to risk a similar fate.

But now she was in the City and Luke had come along and made her rethink her relationship expectations. When he was near her, she felt electricity buzzing between them. The way he looked at her and spoke to her was nothing like what she expected an Exceptional to be. At least, until he was around his friends. Then the cocky, stubborn side of him she saw back at the boundary line came back out. She realized that it should probably bother her, but she found that it heightened her awareness of him.

She didn't go inside until her stomach started to rumble, and even though it was well past breakfast, Mazzi gave her a banana and some toast to eat. Afterward she went up to Luke's room to use his TV since the other Ordinarys were out on errands. She copied the steps she had seen Luke do just yesterday and after a few errors she was able to get a movie playing.

Ally couldn't read the titles or the covers of the movies she chose, so she had to come up with her own summaries. She watched a couple love stories, which peaked her interest based on the inner battle she just experienced in the garden. Back in the settlement love wasn't regarded as serious as it was in these movies. Marriage was important, and many married for love, but it was expected that everyone have a family to help better the community. This meant that sometimes the Ordinarys in the settlement needed to marry someone they could easily get along with, rather than someone he or she loved. Since Ally had tentatively planned on going to the City, love had been lost on her. She didn't know if Ordinarys in the City were allowed to marry, so she had given up that expectation early on.

But the love in these movies made the characters light up. They ran through fields, danced around large rooms full of glamorous looking people, and even gazed at the stars from a blanket on a grassy hill. The stories went on. As Ally watched she couldn't help but be reminded of Luke. She hadn't known him long at all, but she felt comfortable around him. It was as though she had known him all her life, and was really just noticing him now. He seemed to identify her as a person, not just an Ordinary. Ally figured he just felt responsible for her, since it was not likely that an Exceptional would fall for an Ordinary. Things like that only seemed to happen in the movies she was watching, and all that this new world had left was reality.

THAT AFTERNOON ASHER finished his chores early and offered to teach Ally how to play the piano that sat in the foyer. Every time she passed the large, glossy instrument she longed to run her fingers along it. She wanted so badly to hear the music that Sabine said it made. So when they sat down at the small bench behind it and Asher lifted the cover to keys, she quickly reached out and pressed one down. A low note emitted from the back of the piano, echoing through the hall.

Asher laughed at the amazed look on her face and showed her how to position her hands on the keys. She pressed down several notes at once and winced at the unpleasant sound it made.

"It takes practice", he said and put his own hands on the keys.

Ally watched as his fingers glided across the keys, making a melody so perfect she started to sway back and forth.

"It's beautiful," she murmured, continuing to watch his hands. She felt dampness on her cheeks and was surprised when she reached up and felt a tear on her skin. How many other things had she missed out on because of the virus? Or maybe just because she'd been born an Ordinary?

The front door slammed open and Asher stopped playing immediately. Ally peered around the side of the piano and her eyes locked with Luke's. He had dark circles under his eyes, and she could see that his muscles were tensed under his white shirt. He started to climb the stairs and stopped at the railing that looked over the piano.

"How'd it go?" She looked up at him, hoping this was the correct question to ask. She wasn't sure what exactly he had left her to do, but it had seemed important to Luke and his friends.

"I won." His voice sounded stiff. He turned and stomped up the stairs. Ally could hear him walk down the hall and slam his door behind him.

"I should go talk to him." She started to stand but Asher grabbed her arm.

"I wouldn't. He isn't right after a fight. The adrenaline does wacky things to an Exceptional."

She took one last look at the spot where Luke had just stood and nodded her head, placing her hands back on the piano. "Okay, where were we?"

LUKE STAYED in his room that night, which put some confusion in Ally's mind about the morning talk they shared. Rather than over thinking it, she decided to spend the next day getting to know the other Ordinarys in the house.

Sabine taught her how to do the laundry. In the City they had machines that washed clothes for them, so all she needed to do was load and unload the clothes, and then fold them. Back in the settlement they washed their clothes in bins outside their homes, which meant that they had to wash them by hand. The process took a while and in the end, their clothes never seemed very clean.

Flint taught her how to change the filter on the furnace in the basement. Ally hadn't even known the basement existed. It was mainly just for storage, seeming unnaturally damp and cool despite the warm temperatures outside. Flint was a quiet guy, but she was able to gather that he did the handy work around the house.

Asher was able to acquire permission from Mrs. Mathias to take Ally on an errand outside of the house that afternoon. They went to a local food store and picked up ingredients Mazzi needed for cooking the meals. Back in the settlement their food was simple and plain. Meat came from the cattle, chickens, and pigs. Fruits, grains, and vegetables came from the gardens and crops. Sometimes they would buy sugar and other refined items from the City, but not often. Here the Exceptionals could pick from any variety of foods, many of them packaged. Asher explained that the first Exceptionals found and trained workers to run the factories that made the food, trying to keep the City running as normally as possible. Many of them were Ordinarys, and they were required to train their children to follow in their path. Asher's parents had been electricians for the City, and since he was their second son, he was sent to work as a housekeeper.

Luke didn't come home that night, but he did send Ally a message saying that he was sorry he had been busy, and that he would be home the next afternoon to spend time with her. Apparently he had a big test he needed to study for and he chose to stay at Maver's. He decided that being home with her would be too much of a distraction. Ally didn't understand his reasoning; she thought they barely knew each other for her to be considered a distraction.

Since she couldn't read, she had to have Sabine read it to her.

"This is kind of sweet." Sabine giggled as she read it a second time. "I've never seen Mr. Lukin speak to another girl this way. He must really like you."

"He barely knows me." Ally pointed out, folding up the letter and placing it in her nightstand.

"Who says there has to be a time limit on love?" Sabine's face took on a dreamy expression. "You've watched some of Luke's movies, right? Sometimes the people in them know from the first second they lay eyes on each other."

Ally shook her head. "You're crazy. Those are just stories."

Sabine giggled again. "If believing in love like that is crazy, than I am okay not being sane."

Ally shut off the light and rolled over, closing her eyes. Luke had told her that those movies were made-up and that the people in them were called *actors*, or people paid to play those parts. Still, the ideas for them had to come from somewhere. Didn't they?

IT WAS AROUND LUNCHTIME the following day that she received a piece of paper from Mazzi. She recognized it immediately since Sabine, Asher, and Flint received a similar one every morning. It was a work list. She stared at it for a moment and turned to Sabine for help.

Sabine took the paper and read it over. "You're supposed to be at the Institute in an hour. You are to wait in the lobby."

"Did Luke send this?" Ally took the paper from her hands.

"It doesn't say." Sabine shrugged.

Ally laid the paper on the table and took another bite of her sandwich. "Someone will have to take her. She'll never find the Institute on her own." Asher pointed out, looking particularly solemn today.

"Maybe that is part of the task," Sabine said. "She needs to find the Institute on her own and prove her resourcefulness. It doesn't say anything about someone leading her there, and it isn't on any of our work schedules."

Asher rolled his eyes. "You read way too far into those things Sab, but whatever you say."

Ally doubted it was meant to be a test on whether or not she could navigate her way to the Institute. She wanted to head out of the house on her own this time, since her previous excursions had been in the company of another.

"I'll go on my own," she finally said.

After numerous warnings from Sabine that she would need to

70

leave promptly in case she got lost, Ally washed her face in the downstairs bathroom and ran her fingers through her hair to pull out the knots. It was all she had time for. Once she had left the house and was out of Luke's neighborhood, she stepped into the flow of pedestrian traffic headed in deeper into the City. Several Ordinarys passed by with their gazes locked on the street. She could see work lists sticking out of their pockets as they carted around bags of food and piles of paper. Most of the Exceptionals seemed to ignore her completely, but a few gave her stern looks when they caught her looking anywhere but the ground. Sabine had never mentioned this as being something that Ordinarys did, but maybe it was more expected than required.

The crowd thinned out immensely as she walked deeper into the City. The streets become wider, and there were more directions for people to move. She thought about asking someone where the Institute was located but that broke the rule of speaking to an Exceptional first. An Ordinary would have been a better choice, but they all looked caught up in their errands.

Instead she decided to listen to those around her, trying to pick up pieces of conversation. She might not have super hearing, but she could still eavesdrop.

"More and more Ordinarys on the street. What a waste," a male Exceptional said to himself.

Two women Exceptionals walked side by side.

"Did you see Maren's hair-do this morning? So over the top," one of them said.

Another voice popped up to her right.

"I'm on my way to the Institute, we'll catch up later."

Ally's head snapped around, searching for the source of the

71

voice. A male Exceptional finished waving to someone off to his right, and then marched toward a street to the left. She followed him at a safe distance, finding herself in another traffic pattern. Several other Exceptionals were walking a similar path, hopefully headed toward the Institute as well.

Twenty minutes later, and with a few minutes to spare, Ally stepped into the lobby of the Institute. The whole outside of the building had been made with some sort reflective material she had never seen before. The large buildings across from the Institute were reflected so clearly Ally almost believed that she was seeing replicas that had risen across from them. But once inside, the front of the Institute took on a whole new look. Rather than seeing her own reflection in the windows of the Institute, she could now see the people and buildings outside. She turned and peered around the lobby, first noticing that it was several stories high. Directly across from where she stood, she could make out the higher floors, each ending in a balcony that over looked the lobby floor. She was sure there were even more floors past that, but after the fifth floor, the ceiling jutted out over head, made of glass just like the rest of the inner windows.

The lobby of the Institute seemed crowded and Ally wasn't sure how she would ever find Luke. Just to appear productive, she began to weave through the crowd, looking for any Exceptional that might have some resemblance to him. She hoped that since he had asked her to come here, he was searching for her as well.

"You. Ordinary!" A voice barked.

Ally froze in place, recognizing the grinding voice that could only belong to an Exceptional Guard. She turned around to face the fearsome man and tried to appear calm.

72

"I'll need to see your work papers in order to allow you access to this building." He held his hand out and Ally slapped hers to her forehead.

"I left it at home," she said. She thought Sabine might have mentioned bringing her work list along, but Ally had left it sitting on the kitchen table.

"Then I'll need to see you out." He grabbed her arm roughly, cutting off her circulation with his strong grip.

"Wait, I'm meeting someone here." She struggled against him but it was useless.

"Corporal Nicks," a voice boomed. "You can release her."

Ally should have been relieved that she suddenly regained feeling in her arm, but she recognized that voice all too well. She turned and found herself face to face with Aden. He towered over her, crossing his arms over his body.

"I'm glad you got my message."

So the message had been from Aden, not Luke. She hadn't thought about the possibility that he might be at the Institute, but here he stood. Somehow, she didn't think that his reason for bringing her here was backed by good intentions. Ally had pretty good instincts, and right now her arms were tingling with gooseflesh.

"This way." He put his hand on her back and started to move forward. The gesture might have seemed protective coming from anyone else, but Ally found it threatening. They walked across the lobby and stopped in front of a clear shaft that led from the bottom floor to the top. Ally wasn't sure what its purpose was until something large within the shaft glided down toward them and stopped level with the lobby floor. Exceptionals stood inside the box, and when it opened they

73

poured out into the lobby.

When the box was empty, Aden led Ally inside and pushed a button on the wall. Two Exceptional Guards stepped in beside them and stood on either side of Ally. She startled a little when they started to move upward but caught her footing and peered through the front wall, watching the lobby grow smaller as they rose. They finally stopped on the fifth floor, and stepped out into an open hallway. She was then led over to the railing that overlooked the lobby, and she found that Exceptionals appeared just large enough to be recognizable.

Aden peered over the edge as well and focused on something that brought a smile to his lips. He turned to look at her, clasping his hands behind his back in the same moment. "I'm sure you are wondering why I called you here today."

Ally didn't respond, instead avoiding eye contact by continuing to watch the Exceptionals below. She watched as a new group poured out of two large sets of doors. Then, just as she was about to look away, she caught sight of Luke, Pax, and Maver. They stood in the center of the room, looking through some papers they held in their hands. Is that who Aden had been pleased to see below? She wondered if Luke knew she was here. He didn't look around or appear in a hurry.

Aden's hand slammed the rail in front of her and she jumped, turning to face him.

"Why did you bring me here today?" she finally asked.

He shot her a half smile. "My son is hiding something from me, something I need to know. I believe you may know what that thing is."

Ally felt relieved that she could sincerely say, "I have no idea what you are talking about."

Aden's brows furrowed. "You are sure?"

She nodded, wondering why he brought her all the way to the Institute just to ask her this question, and why they were up on the fifth floor to discuss it. Perhaps he was afraid that Luke would spot them in the lobby. Maybe Asher was right, Aden may have been testing her usefulness in getting to the Institute. His first impression hadn't been great.

"Are you a good listener, Ordinary?" He rested a hand on the railing.

"I can be", she said as she held his gaze.

"I think today you'll be a good listener. I'm going to set you up on this railing, and I would ask that you not make noise… just yet."

Ally didn't have time to respond. He grabbed either side of her waist and lifted her as though she weighed no more than a feather. He set her up on the rail and turned her around, forcing her to put her feet over the edge. He kept a hand on her arm, anchoring her to the railing.

The glass windows in the lobby swayed as Ally found herself in a state of vertigo. She had climbed trees with ease, but looking down from five stories up was entirely different. The floor below was hard concrete, and she would smash into pieces once she hit it. For a brief moment she realized this would be a way to end a life of being indentured to Luke and his family, but she wasn't so sure that that she wanted it to end just yet.

"Wh...Why am I up here?" Ally's voice quivered.

"Enjoying the view?" Aden sounded amused and Ally wish she had the courage to spin around and punch him in the face right then and there.

"Not particularly. I could see just fine from where I was standing a moment ago."

"For your own sake, now would be a time to make noise." Aden spoke in her ear, his head so close she could feel his warm breath on her neck. He placed his hand on her back and shoved her off the railing. She screamed out at first and then fell silent, plummeting to the floor below.

Ally had heard that when you are about to die, your life flashes in front of your eyes. She had never really thought about whether this was true, or what moments in her life she would see, but as she fell closer and closer to the ground, one thought was on her mind.

Luke.

Chapter Eight

Luke looked down at Ally, who was now motionless in his arms. He had caught her. He had saved her life. He had heard her scream ring out across the lobby and was able to react in time to catch her. But in the process, he had revealed something about himself that no one else knew. Something he had never planned on sharing.

"Luke?" Her eyes fluttered open and she looked up at him, a confused expression on her face. She peered to either side for a moment, giving Luke a chance to look up. A few Exceptionals that had been too close to him when he had reacted were just picking themselves up off the ground. They hurried away from him and into the crowd.

Aden appeared in the growing empty space around them, clapping loudly. "That was some performance, Luke. My *special* son."

Luke's muscles coiled through his body, and he kept a firm grip on Ally. He wanted so badly to look down and explain things to her, but he couldn't break his gaze with his father.

"You set me up," Luke growled.

"I had no choice." Aden smirked. "You are doing the City a great disservice by keeping your special abilities hidden, son."

"What happened?" Ally managed to croak.

His father seemed perfectly happy to answer this for her. "When Luke saw you fall from the upper level, he rushed forward and saved your life, using a special ability that no other Exceptional his age has."

She looked up at Luke, ignoring the large crowd gathered around them.

"You did?"

Luke answered her through gritted teeth. "Yes."

His father walked over to them, patted Luke on the shoulder, and then stepped back again. "It seems our Luke here can cancel gravity in a small area. Or maybe a large area as well. The details will be discovered with some tests and assessments."

"I don't understand." Ally eyes flitted around the room as she tried to make sense of what had happened.

"You were weightless, and floating above the ground, unable to fall to the ground." Luke finally looked down at her. "When I told you that I had extra abilities, I down played it a little."

Ally cocked her head. "You think?"

"It was magnificent, really." His father beamed at the crowd.

"Don't you think this would be better spoken about at home?" Luke snapped his head up.

"I agree." His father motioned to the Guards behind him. Ally watched as they stepped past him, stopping next to Luke. "But first, your Ordinary here is going to be taken to ORC and checked in."

The whole lobby had been silent until now. The hundred or so Exceptionals began to whisper amongst each other, their eyes on Luke and Ally. He knew his father was going to be upset him with, but he didn't expect this.

"What?" His voice came out almost a gasp.

"Oh, don't worry." His father waved his hand in Ally's direction. "She'll still be yours, but I think it is time she had a proper induction into the City. I also believe that you need some time to sort through your priorities, something I'll be directly overseeing. I'm sure you'll be able to focus much better without this Ordinary around."

Luke's eyes flicked to the Guards standing beside them. After a long moment of suspenseful silence, he set Ally on her feet. The Guards stepped forward and each took one of her arms. She looked back at Luke, her eyes pleading.

"Please, don't let them take me."

He just shook his head, holding his hands out in front of him in apology. "I'll come for you. I promise."

He watched as one of the Guards pulled a silver syringe from a case in his hand. He stepped beside Ally and shoved it into her arm while she was still holding eye contact with Luke. Her eyes rolled up into her head and she collapsed in the Guard's waiting arms. He threw her over his shoulder as though she were nothing more than a doll, and strolled through the lobby and out of sight.

For a moment he thought about going after her, but knew that it would do no good. Several Guards had already stepped forward to block his path. His father cleared his throat and waved his hand, motioning for the gathered crowd to disperse. Conversations restarted and Exceptionals ran to their lessons, for which they could not be late.

"I'll meet you at home." Aden said to Luke, clasping his hands behind his back and walking away.

Luke burst through the doors to the Institute, taking his trip home at full sprint. With his primed Exceptional body, the people around him became blurs as he sped through the streets, arriving home in ten minutes. He burst through the front door, almost pulling it off its hinges. Most homes had been upgraded with stronger materials to withstand the unusual strength of the Exceptionals, but they were not damage proof.

The commotion drew the attention of others in the house. Sabine and Asher made it into the foyer first, followed by his mother, and then Flint and Mazzi. He paced back and forth from the piano to the front door, mumbling to himself.

"Lukin, dear." His mother approached him, reaching her hand out. "What's wrong?"

"Your husband," he spat at her.

"Don't be so dramatic." She pouted her bright purple lips. "What has he done to upset you this time?"

"Don't be dramatic? Really, Mother? He is awful, and you know it. You try to ignore it and pretend that you have a perfect life with a perfect family, but you don't. So, please, stop defending him." Luke regretted the words the moment they left his lips, but the damage was done.

His mother clasped her lips together, fighting the quiver that was running through them. Her garishly painted eyes filled with tears and she swept her robe around, disappearing down the hall and into her office.

"He took Ally," Luke finally said out loud, looking to the remaining people in the room.

Sabine stepped forward. "What? Where?"

"He set me up, and he took Ally. He sent her to ORC. And now she'll know who I am, and why I've brought her here."

"The ORC doesn't change who you are. Ally knows you care about her, I've tried to make it clear," Sabine answered.

"If it wouldn't change anything between us, I would have told her the truth about the ORC from day one. I've had plenty of opportunities." Luke hung his head and then looked up slightly. "Did you really tell her I cared about her?"

She shot him a smile. "Yes, I really did."

He went back to staring at the piano, holding onto the hope that Sabine had just given him. She and Asher eventually slipped out of the room, leaving him to his thoughts. Luke started to pace again, caught between the point of extreme anger and overwhelming sorrow.

The front door opened and his father stepped into the foyer. He glanced at Luke and then walked away from him and into the dining area. Luke followed behind, knowing he had been given a silent command to follow.

His father took a seat at the large dining table and motioned for Luke to do the same. In the only form of rebellion he could think of at the moment, he sat down at the opposite end of the table from his father.

"When were you going to tell me?" Aden folded his hands together on the table.

"Never," Luke answered honestly.

"You would have lied to me for the rest of your life, like you have been lying to me all these years?"

"I never lied. When you asked me about my abilities ten years ago I told you that I could sometimes move objects by raising my palms toward them."

"Yes, but you omitted the best part. You omitted your more powerful ability." Aden struggled to keep his voice calm.

"I didn't think it mattered." Luke shrugged. "How long have you known?"

Aden smirked. "I've suspected it for almost a year now. You've always been so unaffected by my threats and punishments and I was starting to believe I would never find a way to get through to you, until recently. I saw the way you looked at that Ordinary girl when you introduced her to me. You have found someone you truly care about, which means I finally have something to use against you."

"Such a fatherly thing to do." Luke spoke to the table.

"And I'm disappointed in you, Lukin. Your powers will be of such use to us in the future, and they could have been of use to us before now." Aden's face turned into a scowl.

Luke gripped the table, attempting to control his anger. "And if I refuse?"

"Oh, I don't think you will," Aden responded.

"Why is that?" Luke gripped the table.

"I already said that I have something to hold over your head." Aden stood, stepping over to the large computer screen he had hung on the wall for business dinners and meetings. He flipped a switch and a picture of Ally popped onto the screen. She was lying on the white hospital bed, her dark hair fanned out around her. Her eyes were closed and tubes ran into her arms, a monitor beside her bed blinked random numbers off and on.

"What did you do to her?" Luke leaned on the table with the palm of his hands.

"It was such a shame that the Exceptional Guard transporting her gave her a Class A tranquilizer instead of a Class B. He will definitely be punished for his actions." He made a *tsk-tsk* sound with his mouth.

Luke pushed away from the table and charged at his father. "If you hurt her—"

He was stopped mid-run, an invisible force holding him back. He felt his neck compress, as though an invisible rope had been wrapped around it. He clawed at the source, sputtering for air.

Aden, whose hand was raised toward Luke, shook his head. "Did you really think you could bring harm to me? You may have a unique ability, but I am ten times stronger than you will ever be. I identified my powers at a young age and harnessed them, getting into the training center as soon as I was permitted. I was a son a father could be proud of."

The invisible force released Luke and he took a few deep breaths. "What will happen to Ally?"

Aden shrugged. "It depends on how well you cooperate. She is on the brink, floating somewhere between life and death. She can easily be brought back with a quick injection into her IV. But she can also be easily put to sleep, for good."

"All I need to do is cooperate? To go to the training center and learn to use my abilities?" Luke asked.

Aden smiled, but the effort always made him look more menacing. "That, among a few other things."

Luke clenched his jaw, looking up at his father. "I'll go."

THE NEXT MORNING Luke arrived at the Institute early, attempting to seem completely devoted to entering the program. Pax came to the training center three days a week, and to lessons only one day a week. He was training to be an Exceptional solider, and had told stories about the process he had gone through when he first started his program.

Luke would first undergo physical evaluation. The doctors would run tests on his endurance and his statistics in speed, jumping, and so on. He would have his blood drawn as well, so they could study his DNA and see if they could pinpoint the extra ability, although it had yet to be done. Luke figured that Aden had plans to duplicate the most powerful abilities in some sort of serum if he could ever manage to find their source.

The Institute receptionist directed Luke to the elevator, which he was told to take to Level U4. He had forgotten that the training center was underground. Upon exiting the elevator he was greeted by one of the doctors, who must have been alerted to his arrival.

"Good morning Lukin. I'm Dr. Chal. Shall we begin?"

Luke was led into a large, open room where other Exceptionals were already gathered. One young male was moving large metal boxes around without touching them. A female was shooting fire from her palms, aiming at targets set up a dozen yards away from her. He tried to observe more of the occupants but the doctor led him into a smaller room off to the side.

"Before we begin the physical tests, I'd like to see a short preview of what you can do with your abilities. It will give me a better idea of where to begin." Dr. Chal leaned against the desk that was placed on the back wall, lifting his porta-comp to a writing level.

Luke decided this would be an easy test. He raised his hand toward Dr. Chal and focused his mind on the doctor's presence, sensing the space surrounding him. With one thought, he was able to cancel the gravity in a small radius around the doctor. It was almost amusing to watch Dr. Chal startle and yell out as he floated up into the air. He scrambled to grab his porta-comp as it threatened to drift away. Just as easily, Luke released the energy, causing the man to fall back to the ground.

"Sorry, I haven't had the chance to work on landings." In truth, yesterday had been the first time he had used his ability on another human being. He always practiced on objects in his room, being careful enough that no one would discover his secret. Even Pax and Maver didn't know. At least, they hadn't until yesterday.

"That is something we will work on." Dr. Chal straightened his jacket and picked his porta-comp up off the floor. "We'll also work on controlling your ability with just your mind so that you no longer have to use your hands. It helps to disguise your power."

He thought back to how his father had raised his hands in the dining room the previous day. "Does everyone learn to use their ability with out their hands?"

Dr. Chal nodded. "Yes, but many chose to use their hands anyway, thinking it adds style to their abilities."

Luke let out a small laugh. That sounded just like his father.

BY HIS THIRD DAY at the training center, Luke had made significant progress on projecting his ability with out having to reach his hand out. It took more energy out of him when he did, and he was not always successful. Still, Dr. Chal seemed impressed that he had mastered it so quickly, saying it took some Exceptionals months. His father had taken a gamble that day in the Institute, relying on Luke to be in the right place at the right time. If Luke hadn't had such a fast reaction time, that afternoon could have ended very differently. He used that information to fuel the fire burning through his insides, telling him to push himself to be as strong as possible.

Luke continued to excel in his physical tests and the younger trainers came to watch him work, since his ability had never been seen in their time here. Luke wasn't sure why it was considered so powerful. He figured the boy who could move objects, or even the woman that could throw fire from her hands, would be of more use.

At the end of his training session that day, Luke stepped into Dr. Chal's office for his end of the day assessment. The doctor looked over his porta-comp, scrutinizing notes he had taken during the training sessions.

"Why am I so important?" Luke decided to ask. "Is it because Aden is my father?"

Dr. Chal put down his porta-comp and clasped his hands in front of him. "Do you know the full extent of your father's abilities, Lukin?"

Luke rubbed the back of his neck with his hand. "I've experienced a few, seen others, and even heard rumors. I know that he is the most powerful Exceptional in the City, maybe even what remains of the country."

Dr. Chal smiled and nodded. "That is correct. I was a new doctor when your father came into the training center."

Luke hadn't noticed before, but Dr. Chal did show signs of old age. Exceptional bodies didn't break down and wrinkle like Ordinarys, but their hair diminished to a silver color, and their abilities started to weaken.

He continued, "When your father came to see me, his abilities were far less than they are now. Even he was unsure of his use to the City at the time, considering himself the weakest of the trainees."

"Why?" Luke asked.

"Because when Aden first came into the training center, he could only perform one ability. The ability to cancel gravity."

Luke leaned back against the wall, gritting his teeth together and clenching his hands into fists. No wonder his father had been so excited back in the Institute. He had seen a younger version of himself in Luke, and he saw the potential for Luke's abilities. No matter how hard he tried to move in the opposite direction, it appeared that Luke was destined to become just like his father. Because despite what his father was putting him through, despite what he was doing to Ally, Luke couldn't help but feel excited at all of the possibilities.

Chapter Nine

"She's pretty," a female voice said. It sliced through the silence that Ally had found herself trapped in for an undetermined period of time.

"She belongs to Aden's son," a different female voice spoke this time.

Ally tried to open her eyes, finding that her eyelids felt heavy and somehow sealed together.

"I think she is waking up," the first female said.

Ally felt a small hand touch her arm. "Ally? Can you hear me?"

She attempted to open her eyes again and this time she succeeded. She blinked several times as her eyes adjusted to bright light overhead. Two female Ordinarys were leaning over her, assessing her condition.

"I don't believe for one second that that Guard didn't realize he was using an Exceptional tranquilizer on her and not an Ordinary one. He is lucky she didn't die," the female on the right, whom Ally identified as the second female voice she heard, said.

The first female just nodded her head. "I'm sure Aden will make him pay dearly."

Ally wanted to tell them that Aden probably would have been thrilled had she died. He didn't seem to have much interest in her other than using her to gain power over his son, and from what she could remember from after her fall at the Institute, he had gotten his way.

"How long was I out?" Ally's throat was dry so her voice came out extremely hoarse.

"Here, drink some water." The second female held a cup of water up to her mouth. "You've been asleep for four days."

"Four days?" Ally attempted to sit up but the motion made her nauseous. She leaned back onto what appeared to be a small, white bed, and rubbed her head. "Where am I?"

The first female put on a friendly smile. "You're in the infirmary. Now that you're awake, Dr. Hudson will want to see you and make sure you are well enough to receive your own room assignment."

She had hoped for a broader answer, one that explained what building she was in, but it didn't seem like she was going to get it. She had heard Aden mention the ORC, but she still didn't understand what exactly this place was used for. Was she in a hospital of some sort? Maybe an Ordinary processing building or a place for new Ordinarys entering the City?

"We'll get the doctor", the second female said before they both disappeared from the room. Ally closed her eyes again.

A few minutes later a male Exceptional entered the room. He was tall and thin, having to duck down when he stepped through the doorway.

"Glad to see you awake Ordinary J102." He looked down at a small screen in his hand. It looked just like the one a Guard had used to check her into the City. Ally had heard Sabine call it a porta-comp.

"J102?" she repeated slowly.

Dr. Hudson nodded. "Your identification number. Your permanent paper work came in yesterday morning."

She ran her fingers over her wrist and sure enough, the paper bracelet she received when she arrived in the City was gone. Dr. Hudson pulled some metal instruments from the pocket of his white coat and began to check Ally over. Back in the settlement they had a doctor, and he had many of the same instruments, except they were rusted and had been taped together in many places. Dr. Hudson helped her to sit up slowly and this time Ally didn't feel dizzy. He checked her breathing, looked in her ears and mouth, and tested her reflexes.

"Thankfully the tranquilizer did no damage other than putting you to sleep for a few extra days. You seemed to have recovered from the effects well, and the blood panel we did when you first arrived came back normal." Dr. Hudson picked up the porta-comp and pressed a few buttons. "I'll have them come and take you to your assigned room now."

It wasn't long after he left that the two female Ordinarys from earlier returned to the room. They helped Ally off the table and led her out into the hallway. It was long, white, and well lit by large lights hanging from the tiled ceiling. She was led to the left and through a door at the end of the hall. They stepped into another hall just like the other one, except this one had a wide desk at the end. A female Exceptional sat at the desk, watching their approach.

"Wrist please," she said in a malicious voice.

The two females each held out their wrist and the Exceptional scanned their arms. Ally followed suit, surprised when the Exceptional held the scanner over her arm and something beneath her skin lit up blue.

"They implanted your micro-chip yesterday after your paperwork arrived." The first female said as they walked past the desk.

Ally lifted her sleeve and gasped. "My mark. Where is my mark?"

The place where the Oak tree once scarred her skin was now completely bare. Her skin smooth and shiny, as if nothing had ever been there. She ran her finger along the area and felt a small bump under the skin.

"All Ordinarys from the settlements have their marking removed when the micro-chip is implanted. It is a symbol of where you once lived, not where you currently reside. The micro-chip is your new marking", the second female responded.

Ally fought back the tears that were threatening to spill from her eyes. She had never suspected that her mark would be taken away. It was the one thing she had left from home, and now even that was gone.

The next area they entered was best described as a large foyer. Another Exceptional sat behind a desk that was blocked off by a wall of glass. Two hallways ran in opposite directions, and benches filled the open space. Ally followed the females up to the window.

"We have a new Ordinary for processing", the first female said through small holes in the window.

The Exceptional nodded and pressed a button on her desk. Moments later another female Exceptional appeared from the hallway to their right.

"I'll take it from here." She dismissed the two female Ordinarys and Ally watched them disappear back the way they had just come.

"This way, J102." The Exceptional started back down the hallway and Ally jogged to catch up. "My name is Mrs. Hughes. We'll have to stop in processing before I can take you to your assigned room."

They entered a door on the right and entered a large room filled with instruments and beds, just like the room she had just seen the other doctor in. Mrs. Hughes led her to a shower in the back corner of the room.

"Undress and leave your clothes on the floor. You may then enter the shower."

Ally waited for Mrs. Hughes to lead her to a changing area, or at least turn her back, but she did neither. Ally stripped down to nothing, trying not to feel embarrassed as her body was scrutinized.

"In you go." Mrs. Hughes motioned to the shower and Ally stepped in. There were no levers or bottles of soap like at Luke's. She faced the Exceptional and raised her hands in confusion.

Mrs. Hughes pressed a button on the wall and Ally found herself coated in a foamy, yellow substance. It tingled her skin and she instinctively closed her eyes, using her fingers to pinch her nose. A stream of hot water followed the foam, followed by another coat of foam, a stream of cold water, and finally a large dryer that blew the water droplets from her body. Even her hair felt almost dry once the dryer finally turned off.

When she stepped from the shower another Exceptional had arrived in the room. This one braided Ally's hair down her back and helped her dress into clean clothes. These particular clothes were a light yellow color rather than the muted grey she had become accustomed to. Ally was then led to one of the beds in the room and asked to sit on the end. The second Exceptional tied a piece of cloth above Ally's elbow while Mrs. Hughes carried a tray over, lifting a needle into the air.

"I'm going to take some blood. Try not to move."

Ally felt queasy by the time they filled six vials with her blood, and she was given a small cup of something sweet to drink. Whatever it was, Ally felt better almost immediately. Mrs. Hughes asked Ally to follow her, once again, and they stepped back into the hallway.

"You'll be rooming with Ordinary M320," Mrs. Hughes said as they walked.

The identification number didn't mean anything to Ally, but she nodded her head anyway.

"She is from the same settlement as you."

This information peaked Ally's interest.

"Does it say her name? When did she arrive?" Ally's settlement was large, but she knew there was a good chance she might recognize her roommate from home.

Mrs. Hughes shot her an annoyed look. "As I said, M320. When she arrived makes no difference to me, or to you for that matter. You will have time to discuss these details with her yourself once you are settled."

This time when they exited the hallway, they entered a large round room. It was at least fifty yards across. The walls were lined with identical metal doors, and the center of the room held a few tables and some sofas. There was a stairwell to their right that led to up to another metal door, but Mrs. Hughes walked past it and to a door on the far right.

"Room 108." She scanned her wrist on a screen to the right of the door and Ally heard it click open.

Mrs. Hughes pushed the door open and motioned for Ally to enter. She didn't follow her inside, but stood in the doorway.

"Someone will be by to explain the rules and regulations, most likely before dinner time." Mrs. Hughes took one last look at Ally and shut the door. Ally heard a beep and then the sound of the lock turning in the door.

"Hello?" a voice called out from behind her.

She turned slowly, taking in the room that would now be hers. It was long and thin; holding two beds, a sofa, a TV, and minimal decorations. They didn't even have a window. Everything in the room was white, which made the area bright, but Ally found it empty of emotion.

She then found the source of the voice. A female Ordinary sat on the far bed, brushing her flowing blonde hair out of its braid. Ally gasped, leaning against the wall for support.

"Willow?" her voice squeaked.

The girl stood and dropped the brush to the ground. She moved toward Ally and stopped just a few feet from her.

"Ally?" she whispered.

At that moment, whatever had been building up in Ally over the past several days let itself go. She fell to her knees and watched as the tears rolled off her cheeks and splashed to the tile floor below. It took her several minutes to stop crying. Willow kneeled on the floor next to her and rubbed her back, waiting for her to pull herself together. Ally had never been an overly emotional person, but right now she couldn't seem to control her tears.

"Oh Ally," Willow said from beside her. "How did you end up here?"

Ally looked up at Willow. Willow had been her best friend up until six months ago, when she had volunteered to come to the City. Ally was supposed to have volunteered as well, and should have arrived on the caravan with Willow.

"I wasn't sure if I would ever see you again." Ally used the sleeve of her shirt to wipe the tears from underneath her eyes.

Willow smiled. "Come on, let's go to the sofa and talk."

When they were settled into the soft, white cushions, Willow reached over and took Ally's hand in her own.

"Will, I'm so sorry," she said.

Willow held up her hand. "Don't apologize. I never held you to your promise to volunteer. I would have no matter what. We each had to make our own choice, and your family relied on you more than mine did."

Ally swallowed at the lump in her throat, holding back a second round of tears that threatened to spill down her cheeks. "Your family is doing well. Your brother is working closely with Po, just like Stosh. Your mother is still doing laundry, and your father is still a handyman. He fixed our roof this spring when we spouted a leak. He came over and just got up there in the pouring rain."

Willow and Ally shared a laugh.

"That sounds just like him," Willow said, taking a deep breath before she continued. "So, how did you get here, Ally? Did you find a way to track down a Guard and volunteer?"

"Not exactly." Ally looked at her lap. "I was jumping the boundary line."

Willow gasped. "You finally did it?"

They had always talked about someday jumping the boundary line together, with Stosh in tow as well, but that dream had ended when Willow left the settlement. Now Willow would never get the opportunity to experience it, and Ally doubted Stosh would try after what happened to her.

Ally just nodded. "It had seemed so simple at the time. Then the Guards caught me. If I had known they would take me into custody and bring me to the City, I never would have done it."

She filled Willow in on how Luke had come to her rescue in the woods, and the short time she spent in his house, getting to know the other Ordinarys that lived there. She briefly talked about Luke, explaining what she knew about him from their two short talks. She finished with the events at the Institute from a few days ago.

"I just woke up an hour or so ago, and now I'm here." Ally picked at a broken nail on her finger.

"Whoa. I can't believe that you are with Aden's son."

"I wouldn't say with, he is kind to me and all, and part of me even believed he might like me, but we never got a chance to explore that possibility." Ally laughed.

Willow giggled. "To think, my Allona, talking about starting a relationship with a boy. I always thought for sure that you would find a way to avoid getting married. You were such a free spirit, and an Ordinary unwilling to open your heart to love."

Ally felt her cheeks redden, embarrassed to be described that way. Willow knew her so well.

Willow took her hand again. "By the way you are acting, I'm assuming you didn't fulfill the ORC contract."

Ally raised an eyebrow. "The ORC what?"

Willow patted Ally's knee. "Your head must still be foggy from that tranquilizer. The contract, Ally. The one we are held to when an Exceptional chooses us for their service. Since Luke chose you, you must

96

have both signed the contract."

Ally shook her head. "I never signed a contract, but everything happened so fast. I only ever received one assignment and it is the one that put me here."

"No one's told you." Willow's face grew paler and her words came out softly. "You have no idea where you are, do you?"

"No one's told me *what*, Will?" Ally leaned closer to her best friend.

"ORC," she stated the name of the center they were in. "Ordinary Reproduction Center. We're here to be prepared for breeding with Exceptionals."

Before Ally had a chance to respond, a female Exceptional pushed open the door and strolled into the room. She looked Ally and Willow over, a porta-comp held tightly against her chest.

"J102, come with me please." Ally hesitated before getting up, still growing used to her new identification.

Willow gave her a reassuring nod and mouthed, *We'll talk later.*

Ally followed the Exceptional out into the circular room and was led to a room on the other side of the open space. They entered a room that was half the size of the one that Ally and Willow would be sharing. It held only a desk and two chairs. When the Exceptional took a seat behind the desk, Ally took that as a signal to sit down in one of the chairs.

A computer sat to the side and the Exceptional studied it. They had one computer back in the settlement, but it was slightly older and no one was allowed to touch it except for Po. The City had given it to him so that he could enter the wood production numbers, and send messages if he needed to. Sometimes he received messages from Aden, which he then relayed to everyone in the gathering hall.

"I see you are already under contract, which makes this somewhat easier. We have a signature from Mr. Lukin Mathias, so we'll just need one from you." The Exceptional clicked a button on the computer and a piece of paper printed from a device that sat on the floor. "I doubt you even know how to write."

Ally tried to overlook how offensive that comment was. "You are correct."

"Do you, Ordinary J102, give me the authority to sign this document for you?" The Exceptional sounded bored.

"Do I have a choice?"

"Not really."

"Then go ahead," Ally sighed. "Will you at least tell me what it says?"

The Exceptional looked annoyed that she had to answer a question. "Basically, your specific contract says that at a time of his choosing, Mr. Lukin Mathias will come to collect you from ORC. You will then live with him, fulfill your breeding duties, and hopefully produce one or more healthy children. Some Ordinarys are required to return to ORC after, but your contract specifically says that you will live out the remainder of your time in the City with Mr. Lukin Mathias."

"Sounds fun," Ally mumbled.

"Until then," the Exceptional's voice rose exceedingly, "you will be required to follow the rules put in place by the leaders and staff here at ORC. Each morning the schedule will be read out loud over the loudspeaker, and you will be required to follow it. You will also need to be on time. Always. Ordinarys here at ORC are kept on a strict diet, and are required to exercise to keep their bodies in the best health possible for reproduction. You will receive weekly tests to check your vitamin levels, and to assess your health at the time. If you follow these rules and stay out of trouble, things will be very nice for you here. Mr. Lukin Mathias is an outstanding Exceptional prospect, you are lucky to have him choose you."

Ally's tongue felt heavy in her mouth. *Lucky?* She wanted to run back to her room and see Willow. She needed to talk about this with someone who was in a similar position, not an Exceptional.

"I'll escort you back to your room now. Dinner will be served to you there."

As soon as the Exceptional locked Ally back in her room, Ally took a few deep breaths. Willow was back to sitting on her bed, brushing through her blonde hair again. She had the TV on and it was playing a romance Ally remembered seeing in Luke's movie collection.

"They only give us romance movies." Willow pointed at the screen. "I think it is to train us for what's to come. Some of them are really graphic."

Ally frowned. "I don't think romance is the foundation for what happens here."

Willow shrugged.

Ally sat next to her on the bed. "Will, are you under contract?"

Willow set down her brush and looked at her hands. "Yes. I'll be leaving sometime in the next few weeks, but I'll return once I fulfill my requirements."

Her passive attitude scared Ally. "And you are okay with that?"

Willow rolled her eyes. "I shouldn't be, but I am having trouble being upset over it."

"How has no one in the settlements ever heard of ORC?"

"Probably because any Ordinary that passes through the walls to the City never comes back out. And you know those Exceptional Guards aren't going to talk about it."

Ally nodded her head. "Are there males here as well then?"

"Not that I've seen." Willow thought about it.

A thought dawned on Ally. "Sabine, Asher, and Flint. They said they were born in the City, maybe they are products of the ORC."

Willow shook her head. "If they are Ordinarys, I doubt it. Did you know that any child with at least one Exceptional parent will be Exceptional as well?

"Really? Interesting." Ally tapped her fingers on the bed.

"Can you imagine me pregnant? And with an Exceptional baby no less. I'd kind of like a little girl," Willow said suddenly.

Just a year ago Ally and Willow had talked about how they would put off marrying as long as possible. Babies had never been on their mind. Now Willow was talking as if she might be pregnant in the next month or two. In actuality, she very well could be.

"Why are they using us for breeding?" The concept didn't seem rational considering there were plenty of Exceptionals that could breed with each other. And Ally assumed that the Exceptionals would want to ensure that their offspring would inherit their supposedly superior DNA. Luke had said that Exceptional powers had evolved to be stronger over time, so would an Exceptional baby from an Ordinary start back at the bottom without a pure genetic line?

A kissing scene on the TV had momentarily caught Willow's attention, but she quickly turned back to Ally. "I guess I've never thought about it."

"Luke is going to come and get me, Will, and when he does I'm going to have him take you with us as well." Ally squeezed Willow's hand.

"Whatever you say," Willow said before returning her attention to the movie.

Chapter Ten

That night dinner came in the form of plain chicken, steamed broccoli, and grainy bread. The Exceptional hadn't been lying when she said that their diets would be healthy and monitored. After they had eaten and placed their plates back through a slot in the bottom of the door, Willow's mood changed dramatically. She became withdrawn and drowsy, saying that she just wanted to go to bed. She couldn't even seem to remember what they had been talking about before dinner. Despite being asleep for four days, Ally still felt tired and had no issue falling asleep quickly in her new bed.

The next morning Ally rose before Willow and took a shower. Even though she had just taken one the night before, she felt dirty just by being in this place. Slowly but surely, as the warm water washed over her, she could feel pieces of the old Ally coming back to life. She never handled being contained well. If she had known that coming to the City would mean lack of fresh air, she never would have even considered it.

By the time she was out of the shower and dressed, Willow was up and moving around their room. Her mood had improved since the night before, and she even joked with Ally about how sunny they looked with their yellow clothes. Their clothes back in the settlement had been black as night, and that contrast was humorous in itself. Especially considering that sunshine brought with it an air of happiness, and Ally felt none of that in this place.

A speaker over their door crackled to life. "Breakfast in five minutes."

The door clicked open and Ally followed Willow out into the common area. It was a much different atmosphere than the last two times she had walked through it. Other female Ordinarys were trickling out of their rooms and into the open space, greeting each other with hand signals. Several were already seated at the tables, holding conversations with each other. She followed Willow to a table near the middle, where two other girls were already seated.

"This is Ally. She just arrived last night," Willow said as she sat down. Ally followed her lead and lowered herself onto the bench.

The girls smiled slightly and went back to talking quietly. Ally had a feeling that the girls in here were anything but friendly, and she didn't blame them. This wasn't what they had expected when they volunteered to come to the City, and each new Ordinary was just another reminder of the friends and family they had left behind. She wouldn't be surprised if they felt resentful at the thought that she might have recently volunteered, when most might do anything to take the same action back.

After a breakfast of eggs, fruit, and more of the same grainy bread from last night, the girls on the first floor were shuffled into a large room filled with chairs. An Exceptional stood at the front of the room and talked to them about their reproductive cycles, and methods for achieving pregnancy. Ally's mind felt foggy again, as if she had just been lifted from yet another drug induced sleep. She found that she could focus on what the Exceptional was teaching them, but not much else. She couldn't seem to recall anything from outside these walls. The other Ordinarys seemed to be in a similar state, a sea of yellow all staring toward the front of the room.

From their lessons they moved on to exercise. They were taken into a large gym and made to walk around the perimeter for thirty minutes. They spent the next thirty minutes doing exercises that worked all of their body muscles. They then had free time until lunch, and after lunch they had two more lessons before being sent to their rooms for the remainder of the day. The last two lessons focused on reading and writing, which Ally was actually grateful for. If she was going to be held in this awful place, at least she could get something worthwhile from it.

The schedule repeated itself the following day. She didn't talk with the other girls much, although Willow would try to include her in conversation sometimes. It wasn't Willow's fault that she wasn't fitting in; she couldn't seem to allow herself to invest in new friendships. Everything about the ORC was wrong. She was sure that Ordinarys in the old world never had a place like this.

Also in repetition was the foggy feeling she experienced several times a day. During those times she remembered less and less about what she had experienced before the ORC, and one morning she caught herself wondering if she had ever lived anywhere else at all. Sometimes, after a headache inducing concentration, she found that she could work her way through the veil that shielded her from her prior memories. There were times during the day where she could recall her previous life with ease, and she noticed that the other Ordinarys shared her moments of clarity around the same time. On the third day, Ally had formed a theory about why she was feeling so off, and took steps to counteract it. She only hoped that it wasn't too late to reverse any damage that may have been done to her.

ON HER FIFTH DAY in the ORC, they received two new Ordinarys to their floor. Neither girl was from the same settlement she and Willow came from, and both looked frightened and confused. They refused to talk their first day, spending their time sulking in the corner of the common room. On the second day one girl had a break down and tried to use a classroom chair to break through the large metal door the Exceptionals used to access their floor. Two Exceptional doctors had to hold her down while a third injected her with tranquilizer. She didn't return to the floor after that.

That same afternoon Ally was taken from the floor for her first evaluation. She was led through the same hall that brought her here, and back into the same exam room. She was made to shower in the fluffy foam again, and had more blood drawn. Dr. Hudson stepped into the room, and Ally was slightly surprised to see him.

"Your blood work is still normal, but we are slightly worried about a sudden dip in your weight. Have you been eating?" He looked up at her.

"I haven't had much of an appetite since coming here," she answered.

"Completely normal," he said, as though she were mourning the loss of a family member and not upset over being imprisoned. "Try to keep up with your calorie requirements for the day. If you haven't made improvements by the time your next assessment comes around, we'll need to put a feeding tube in."

That sounded just about as much fun as some of the topics in their Reproduction lessons. Dr. Hudson left the room quickly, failing to say goodbye. The female Exceptional who had retrieved her from her lessons reappeared to take her back to the common area. She was

105

starting to wish they wore identification of some sort, so that she could recognize them better.

She made it back just in time for the last half of her writing class. When she sat down Willow leaned over her desk and whispered, "How did it go?"

"Took a shower. Had some blood drawn. Was told I need to eat more." Ally shrugged.

Willow nodded her head. "Weight loss is to be expected."

Ally stiffened and peered over at her friend, who was copying a sentence from the board onto the piece of paper in front of her. All of the other girls were doing the same, their faces tense with concentration. It had been this way since Ally had arrived at the ORC. The girls on her floor moved from lesson to lesson, activity to activity, with no sign of resistance or annoyance. Had Ally looked just like this with her foggy mind? She had formed a theory just two days prior, and it appeared to be working so far. The less she ate, the clearer her mind felt.

That night back in their room, Ally and Willow sat down to eat another dinner of baked chicken, brown rice, and carrots; the vegetable of the day. She and Willow had normal conversation to start, but the more Willow ate, the stranger she acted. Ally barely touched her food, taking only a few bites and keeping them several minutes apart. She ate evenly between the three options, not sure if there was something in each item or just one. As usual, as soon as their plates were through the slot in the door, Willow crawled into bed and fell asleep quickly. Whatever they were given at dinner seemed stronger than the other three meals, since none of the Ordinarys were falling asleep during lessons or exercise.

The next day, during their Reproduction lesson, Ally probed deeper into her theory. Their instructor, who still had yet to introduce herself, was talking about changes the body went through in the different stages of pregnancy.

Ally raised her hand, which startled the instructor. All of other girls always remained quiet, listening to her speak. When Ally had been feeling foggy, she never would have thought to ask a question.

"Yes, J102," the instructor said after looking at her porta-comp, most likely trying to identify which Ordinary was speaking. All heads were turned to where Ally was seated.

"Could certain substances, say a pill of some sort, hinder one's chance at becoming pregnant?" Ally tilted her head, trying to appear somewhat dazed.

The instructor set her porta-comp back on the desk. "It depends on the substance. Most are harmless when it comes to fertilization, and if stopped when conception happens, the pregnancy should be able to continue without complications."

The instructor ended her explanation by picking up where she had left off, letting Ally know that question and answer period was over. But Ally had seen the twitch in the instructor's lips as the question left her mouth. She was on to something, but she secretly wondered if her curiosity would get her into trouble.

The days rolled by and Ally lost count of how long she had been in the ORC. Willow seemed more and more distant with each day, and one night after dinner she barely recognized Ally. Ally determined that Willow had been so aware when she first arrived because it was something new and exciting from home. Once the adrenaline wore off, Willow went back to her current state of dazed stupor.

While the days grew longer, Ally grew thinner, still refusing to touch most of her food. She had another assessment coming up, and surely they would put a tube in her, as Dr. Hudson had put it. Then they could pump any drug they wanted into her, and she wouldn't be able to do anything about it.

The day before her assessment, just before breakfast, an Exceptional strolled into their room. She held paperwork in her hand and announced that Willow would be leaving with her matched Exceptional tonight. Willow packed up a few pairs of clothes and her hairbrush, hesitating by the collection of movies that she would be required to leave behind. She stopped in front of Ally before leaving, wrapping her in a big hug.

"Stay safe," she whispered in Ally's ear.

"You too", Ally responded. She smiled at the hint that there was still some of the old Willow left in the blonde, female shell she had been living with.

When dinner came that night, Ally left it sitting on the floor. Someone had delivered two plates, not realizing that Willow was no longer there. Ally thought that was awfully unorganized for this Exceptional establishment, but maybe they were hopeful that she would partake in eating from both plates. Instead, Ally paced the room for a while, feeling as if her life were falling to pieces by the day. Her only hope now would be for Luke to come and retrieve her. Once she was on the outside she could find Willow, and hopefully keep her from being sent back to the ORC. Maybe the dazed personality Willow had taken on would wear off by then.

THE NEXT DAY at breakfast, the others slowly noticed Willow's absence. Ally had seen two girls disappear in her time here and there always seemed to be a silent mourning period. The girls didn't spend much time interacting, or even forming strong friendships, but they understood the circumstances in which their fellow floor mates were being taken.

Ally sat down with the two girls she met her first morning on the floor. They sat with each other for breakfast and lunch; dinner was always served in their respective rooms. She still didn't know their names, and they didn't know hers either. Based on lessons, she knew that the girl on the right was J203 and the girl on the left was A024. Just a number to the Exceptionals. Always.

J203 leaned forward slightly. "Did Willow finally get an assignment?"

Ally just nodded, not wanting to talk about it. She had trouble falling asleep last night, and when she did she dreamt of Willow. The room felt too big without Willow there to occupy half the space. Ally didn't even have to wait for the shower last night, or worry that watching a movie would wake her best friend.

A024 picked at a dried piece of food on the table. "At least she is fulfilling her purpose. It's better than rotting away in this place."

"At least in here she is safe," Ally mumbled.

What she meant was that Willow was safe as long as they were together. In the ORC, Ally could look after her. But out in the City, she had no idea where Willow had been taken or what was being done to her. She had an idea, but she didn't want to dwell on that thought for longer than necessary.

Ally thought back to how she had felt safe during her time with Luke. Life was moving along just fine despite her purpose for being there, which she hadn't even known yet. She even had a few friends. She wondered how Sabine, Asher, and Flint were doing. How had they interpreted her disappearance? Had they been told anything? Surely they had known her reason for being there, and they had neglected to tell her. Perhaps they thought she already knew and just didn't want to speak of it.

"J102," a voice boomed over the speaker." All of the girls jumped. "J102, please report to the main door and wait for further instruction."

"Maybe you are getting your assignment as well," J203 said. "That was fast."

Ally shrugged. "Apparently I had a contract before I even stepped foot in the City. He must be here to collect."

Mrs. Hughes met her at the door. "Mr. Mathias is here to see you. You can gather your belongings and meet me back at this door."

Ally froze. Did Mrs. Hughes mean Aden or Luke when she said Mr. Mathias? She swallowed back the lump forming in her throat and held her head high.

"I didn't come with any belongings," Ally responded. "And there is nothing here that I would want to keep."

Mrs. Hughes shrugged and stepped into the hall, leading Ally back the way she had come when she first arrived here. She wasn't sure what, or who, waited for her at the other end of the hall, and she started to mentally prepare herself for several different situations. It could mean further incarceration, or freedom, and Ally found herself vocally wishing for the latter. She didn't care that Mrs. Hughes shot her a dirty look over her shoulder; Ally just wanted this all to be over.

Chapter Eleven

Luke was surprised that his father had given him permission to bring Ally home from the ORC so soon. He had worked hard during his three weeks at the training center, making considerable progress. One of the trainers had even mentioned that he was advancing faster than Aden ever had, but Luke couldn't tell his father that. Aden might want powerful men in his circle, but one thing he definitely didn't want was anyone more powerful than himself. Still, it had seemed almost too easy.

He had only ever been in the ORC once, four years ago, and it wasn't by choice. His father had dragged him into the building and forced him to look over a line-up of young Ordinary girls, all chosen for their prime physical appearance and almost perfect genes. He still had two years before he would be allowed to even put in a request for an Ordinary, but his father had wanted him to preview what it would be like. He remembered that day and their conversation well.

"Why do I have to choose an Ordinary for reproduction? Or for my wife?" Luke had asked.

"The second part is optional, Lukin." Aden had avoided his question. "But the City needs to see you behind this."

Luke had turned back to the girls lined up against a blank white wall, their faces void of emotion. "They look so sad. Why do we do this again?"

Aden had taken Luke's shoulders and turned him so that they were face to face. "Because we do. We never question the laws that the City has in place. Do you understand?"

Luke had nodded quickly in response. He had been told the same thing his whole life, at home and at the Institute. The City laws are absolute. Do not question them. Do not go against them. If you follow them, the City will prosper.

They had left the ORC immediately after that, but Luke's father had pressured him multiple times over the next several years, urging him to go and choose an Ordinary as his own. If it hadn't been for Luke's mother stepping in to defend him, he may have had no choice but to choose an Ordinary the day he turned sixteen.

Now he sat at a table in a similar room, waiting for one of the ORC staff members to bring Ally to him. He was anxious to take her home today, but nervous as to how she would react to seeing him. She knew the truth now, but still hadn't heard his side of the story. When the door finally opened, he jumped up from his chair, watching as Ally stepped into the room.

Her dark hair hung loosely behind her back, appearing stringy and knotted around her face. Her usually sparkling green eyes were dull, and black circles were shaded beneath them. She also appeared thinner, as if she hadn't eaten since she arrived here. It brought back more memories of his previous visit to the ORC and of the blank faces on the girls he had seen.

"Ally…" he started.

She walked toward him briskly, and for a second he thought she might hug him, but instead she reared her hand back and slapped him across the face. The strike didn't hurt, but his cheek vibrated around the spot where she had hit him.

"I deserved that", he said.

She pointed a finger at him, bringing her hand up so quickly he stepped back. "You deserve much worse than that, Lukin."

She said his full name with distaste.

"Ally, if you'll just let me explain..." he pleaded with her.

"I don't want your explanations!" she yelled, pacing the room. "I figured things out just fine on my own."

He stood there motionless; waiting for her to finish whatever rant she was about to go on.

"Take me out of here, Luke." She stopped walking and turned to look at him. For a moment, her mood softened and her eyes pleaded with him. "I need fresh air."

He nodded and stepped toward the door. He thought about taking her hand, or just offering her his arm, but something in her eyes said his face might suffer from the gesture. She followed him out into the small check-in area and he handed over the paperwork from his father. He knew there was certain procedures the Ordinarys underwent before leaving, but before seeing Ally he had argued with one of the heads of the ORC, finally gaining permission to bypass them all.

A female Exceptional walked them through the hallways, into the main lobby of the ORC, and left them once they were near the exit doors. Luke opened the door for Ally, and once outside, she relaxed a little. She took a few breaths of fresh air and turned her face up toward the sky, letting the sun wash over her face. Just when he thought she might stand there all day, she stalked off toward a side street.

"Ally", he called out. "Ally, wait."

He caught up and grabbed hold of her arm, which caused her to spin around and raise her hand high in a threatening position.

"We don't have to talk right now. It's just that, well, you are going in the wrong direction," he said, letting go of her arm and holding his hands out to claim innocence.

Her eyes narrowed and then she motioned for him to lead her forward. It seemed as though he would be receiving the silent treatment for the time being. It might take some time, but he knew that she would eventually trust him again. Until then he could openly blame his father for this situation.

ALLY HAD A WELCOMING COMMITTEE waiting for her when they stepped into the house. Sabine ran forward and gave her a big hug, while Asher and Flint squeezed her shoulders, welcoming her home with words of greeting. Luke knew he was losing his chance to talk to Ally, and he needed to speak with her before she shut him out completely. Even if she refused to respond, she could still listen.

"Don't you have work lists to be completing?" he said to the others, hoping they would get the hint. Asher and Flint hurried from the room but Sabine was slower to move on.

"I do have some laundry to do," she said.

"I'll help." Ally jumped the chance to leave and started to follow Sabine toward the kitchen.

Luke focused his mind on Ally's presence, zoning in on the space around her. With more ease than he had exhibited a week ago, he was able to lift her into the air and leave Sabine completely untouched.

"Hey!" Ally cried out.

Sabine turned and shook her head at Luke. By now she had heard about his new abilities and didn't seem phased by the sight of them, but he could sense the disapproval in her look.

"That will be all." He glared at Sabine, who finally turned and disappeared into the kitchen.

"Is this what you are resorting to now? Using your abilities to get what you want?" Ally floated in mid-air, managing to keep her gaze locked with his.

"If it will make you listen to me", he said. Using abilities to control Ordinarys was something his father might do, but not Luke.

Her eyes narrowed. "If you put me down, I'll hear you out. But after that I want you to leave me alone."

It was odd, receiving orders from an Ordinary. The others followed a strict "do not speak unless spoken to rule," and it was rarely broken. Luke wasn't even sure that he had ever heard many Ordinarys speak outside of their homes at all. They normally walked with their eyes trained on the ground and their mouths tightly closed. He was learning quickly that Ally was anything but ordinary.

He walked over to her and placed his hands on her shoulders, righting her stance before he set her back on the ground. "I'm still working on replacing objects once I've cancelled gravity around them. I've knocked a few doctors and trainees around in the past few weeks."

His humor was lost on her as she easily maneuvered her way out of his grasp. "Let's talk in the garden, I've spent enough time indoors."

They made their way back to the fountain and sat down on the same bench they sat on just a few weeks ago. Luke wished he could go back to that moment in time. He would set aside his ego and either forfeit or postpone the challenge with Tighe. Maybe then he would have finally told Ally the truth, and she would have been more prepared going into the ORC. He now had no doubts that Aden had planned on sending her there one way or another.

"Ally." He fought the urge to reach out and take her hand. "I need you to know how sorry I am."

"Tell me what you know." Ally ignored his apology. "About the breeding program at the ORC. What did you know before you even met me?"

Luke had been preparing himself for this question for the past three weeks, but even now the words struggled to come out. "All Exceptional males are required to conceive a child with at least one Ordinary female from the ORC. We are allowed to start our contracts at the age of sixteen, and have until we are twenty-one to complete them."

Ally sneered at him. "And you see no issue with this?"

"I didn't before. We don't question the laws of our leaders," he answered truthfully. "It was never appealing to me, and I had planned on holding out as long as possible, but then you came along."

"That part at least makes sense to me." Ally cut in. "Why you were so kind to me when you brought me to the City. Why you acted so interested in me. And to think, I was really starting to change my view on relationships. Then I got to the ORC and realized that I had just been another part of your Exceptional lifestyle. Another requirement for you."

"That isn't true." Luke spun on the bench and faced her.

"Isn't it? Did you not claim me knowing the purpose I would have to you?" She locked her gaze on something across the garden, refusing to look at him.

"Yes, I knew what it meant when I claimed you. I understood what would be expected of me, of us", he said.

"But to treat Ordinarys this way?" Ally gave him a quick glance. "In the settlements we are conditioned from the beginning that we are less than Exceptionals. We are told that if we wish to, one day we can

116

come to the City and work for them, and that it would be considered a great honor. Instead you are forcing Ordinary girls into the ORC and treating them like animals. Work assignments is one thing, but forcing them to breed with Exceptionals goes against human nature. There is no honor in that. You Exceptionals may consider yourselves special, but us Ordinarys hold on to all the good that is left in this world."

Luke let the full force of her words hit him. "You're right, Ally. And I need you to know, I never intended to hold you to a contract, or rush through the process."

"What did you intend to happen then?" she muttered as she kicked a stray rock with her foot.

"I was hoping that maybe, if it were meant to be, you would feel for me what I felt the first time I laid eyes on you, that first day in the woods. You were coming to the City whether I stepped forward or not, but the difference is that I have given you a choice. I've required nothing more than companionship from you since then. I *chose* you that day in the woods because I couldn't bear the thought of you being with someone else."

Ally finally looked up at him. "And how do I know you're telling the truth? How do I know you aren't making this up?"

"I guess that is something you'll have to decide for yourself." He stood and walked away from her, following the winding path that led to the house. He had said what he could, and he was grateful that Ally had even listened to him. Now, it was up to her to decide if and when she would forgive him.

Chapter Twelve

Ally watched Luke leave the garden and enter the house, his words playing over and over again in her head.

"I was hoping you would feel for me what I felt the first time I laid eyes on you."

"I've given you a choice."

Yes, but between the lesser of two evils.

And the words that weighed on her the heaviest of all.

"I chose you that day in the woods because I couldn't bear the thought of you being with someone else."

She eventually made her way back into the house and paused in the kitchen. Sabine sat at the table, folding a large white shirt.

"Ally?" Sabine dropped the shirt and stood. "Is he gone now?"

Ally could only manage a nod.

"Why don't you sit? Mazzi is going to make us some snacks."

Ally smiled and took a seat. She and Sabine hadn't known each other long, but Ally couldn't help but feel as though she had a friend again.

"Well, look at you." Mazzi's eyes widened as she stepped from the pantry. "Did they even feed you there?"

Ally had forgotten about the weight loss. Her hair had to be a mess as well. A long, hot shower would help restore her later tonight, but for now she wanted to sit with the others and hold normal conversation.

"Yes, but nothing as good as your food Mazzi."

The cook smiled and went back to work on preparing whatever

fancy snack she had in mind for this afternoon. Asher and Flint joined them minutes later, trying to look anywhere in the room except at Ally.

"Do I really look that bad?" Ally laughed.

"No," Flint said.

"Yes," Asher said at the same exact time.

Now the four of them laughed together, and Ally realized then how much she really had missed the company of friends. Yes, Willow had been, and still was, her friend. But the Willow that Ally knew back in the settlement was much different than the dazed, drugged out one she has been with in the ORC.

"We are glad you are back," Sabine said. "Mr. Lukin has been moping around the house for the past three weeks. And every time Mr. Mathias came home from the office the two of them would stand in the dining room and argue. I started saving all of my errands for the evening so I wouldn't be here to listen to them."

Ally pulled her feet up onto the chair and wrapped her arms around her knees. "Was it really that bad?"

Asher nodded, looking hesitant to admit it. "Sabine is right, Ally. Luk- I mean Mr. Lukin really cares about you. It has been very apparent."

Ally picked at the wood grain on the table. "I'm having trouble processing what happened to me at the ORC. I've been blaming Luke since the moment that I learned the purpose of that place. Like I told him, Ordinarys have grown accustomed to serving the Exceptionals as workers, but not as breeders. It isn't right."

Sabine took a deep breath. "Can I give you another perspective?"

Ally raised her eyebrow. "You aren't going to justify the ORC, are you?"

Sabine shook her head. "Not intentionally. But Ally, did you ever think about it from Luke's end? Like we've been conditioned to work for Exceptionals, they've been similarly conditioned that all we are good for is work and breeding. They don't view it as wrong because no other Exceptional does, and if someone happens to find it wrong, they have never spoken up. From a young age they are told to accept the laws of our City. Luke has never been given a reason to doubt the ORC. That is, before you came along."

Ally froze in her seat, her eyes meeting Sabine's gaze. "I don't know why I didn't see it that way before."

It was true. Everything Sabine had said. Luke had looked awful when she first saw him in that meeting room, with dark circles under his eyes and a dejected expression on his face. Perhaps he had been suffering in his own way while she was in the ORC.

Sabine smiled. "Sometimes all you need is some group conversation."

Ally squeezed her friend's hand and then sighed. "I still can't stomach the idea of the ORC. I want nothing more than to have that place shut down."

"Keep your ideas to yourself." Sabine leaned toward her. "You have a good thing going here. Mr. Lukin cares for you, and since you are his contract, no other Ordinary can touch you with out his permission. As long as you are in this family, you are safe."

Ally let out a small laugh. "Am I?"

After they ate their snack and the others dispersed to finish their work lists, Ally headed up the stairs and straight into the bathroom. She ran the water hotter than usual and stripped out of her yellow clothes,

120

dumping them into the trash. She didn't care if it was a waste, she
didn't want to own anything from the ORC. After a shower long enough
to prune her fingers and her toes, she finally stepped out and wrapped
herself in a towel. She took a brush from the cabinet next to the sink and
pulled it through her hair until all of the knots were gone.

Ally looked at the mirror. She took in how her collarbone jutted
out above her chest and how the spaces underneath her eyes were tinted
a deep purple color. She turned away from the image in the mirror
quickly; not wanting to stare at the damage that horrible place had done
to her appearance. She set the brush back in its place and walked to her
room, grabbing a fresh pair of clothes from the drawer. She lifted them
to her nose and smelled them, taking in the familiar scent of Luke's
home. It was oddly comforting.

By the time she was ready to leave her room, she had already
decided what she needed to do. The hall felt longer than usual as she
walked toward Luke's room, her bare feet sinking into the plush carpet.
She raised her hand and knocked lightly on his door, willing her heart to
slow down. Luke's Exceptional ears could certainly hear it's eager
beating on the other side of the door.

"I already told you Mazzi, I don't want any food!" Luke's voice
yelled from the other side of the door.

"It's Ally", she responded.

She heard something bang in Luke's room and in a few seconds
he opened the door. Ally had to contain her shock when he stepped into
the open space. He stood there shirtless, the hard lines of his muscled
body exposed to her. She was used to seeing similar bodies back in the
settlement, since the woodcutters often worked shirtless, but Luke's body
had a different effect on her. He held a book under one arm, which told

her that he had probably been sitting on the sofa reading when she knocked.

"Hey." The nervous tone to his voice said that he hadn't expected to find her standing in his doorway, and she hoped that kept him from noticing her reaction to him. "Come in."

She stepped into his room slowly, waiting as he closed the door behind her. She had been in here once before, on her first full day in the City, and it looked exactly the same. Clothes and books were still strewn about the floor, and the large bed against the left wall was unmade.

"Luke." She rubbed her hands together nervously. "I want to apologize."

He placed the book on the dresser near the door and faced her, his eyes wide with surprise. "Why are *you* apologizing?"

"Sabine said something to me, downstairs, and it has stuck with me for the past hour. It isn't your fault that the ORC exists, and it isn't your fault that you've never questioned it. You are only doing what you you've been told to do. I am still upset that you didn't tell me about the ORC from the beginning though, and I wish you would have just been honest with me. At least then I wouldn't have spent the past few weeks completely resenting you."

Luke stepped toward her. "Trust me, I wish I would have told you as well. I had planned to, but chickened out at the last minute. I thought maybe it wouldn't matter, since you probably wouldn't be going there anyway, but as usual my father managed to come along and screw things up."

"What happened that day at the Institute, after they took me away?" Ally hadn't forgotten about her fall from the fifth floor and how Luke had saved her life. Much of what had happened at the ORC in the past two to three weeks had overshadowed it, but the memory of that afternoon was still fresh in her mind.

"I started my training immediately." Luke sat on the edge of the bed and patted the spot beside him. She sat down carefully, keeping some space between their bodies, even if it was small.

"You seemed to have pretty good control earlier, when you lifted me into the air."

He nodded. "I'm lucky that I was able to catch you that day in the lobby. I had never used my abilities on anything other than inanimate objects before. I think it was pure adrenaline mixed with fear that made me so successful. My father told me that if I wanted you to come home from the ORC, I would need to prove to him that I could control my abilities and harness them into something great. He needed to see dedication from me, so that is exactly what I gave him."

Ally was having trouble controlling her feelings as she listened to him speak. Her hands felt clammy just from watching him, and she felt an inexplicable urge to reach out and touch him. She knew she would be angry when she was reunited with him, but what she least expected was to come to a realization of how much she had missed him. And how much she wanted to be with him.

"Why are you staring at me like that?" He laughed. "You look like you might faint at any moment."

"We are a lot like that couple in the book your mom showed me." She said suddenly.

"What book?" Luke's expression was genuinely confused.

"I'll show you." She took his hand, thankful for a reason to touch him, and led him out of his room and down the stairs. Once they were in the library she began to search for the book, pretty sure she remembered which shelf it was on. After pulling the wrong book twice, she finally found it on the third try.

"This one." She showed him the cover. "Your mother said that it is about two people who fall for each other despite the differences in their family. That is kind of like us, except that our differences are that I'm Ordinary and you are Exceptional."

Luke gave her a crooked smile. "You're falling for me?"

She rolled her eyes. "Is that what this book is really about? I couldn't tell if she was being serious or not."

"Why don't you read it and find out." He tapped the cover with a single finger.

"I can't read, I thought you knew that." She opened the cover and stared at the scribbles on the page.

He took the book from her. "Well, I guess I could read it to you."

"Just tell me if I'm right."

Luke looked up at her and smiled. "Yes, it is about a forbidden love."

"And do they really die in the end?" She recalled that part of his mother's summary the most. "Because of their love for each other?"

He nodded. "They do, but more from their own stupidity. The girl fakes her death but the boy misinterprets it and kills himself. When she finds out that he actually killed himself because of her, she ends up stabbing herself with a knife. In the end, their families come together and agree to get along, but it is still very tragic."

Ally wrinkled her nose. "Yeah, I think I'll pass on you reading it to me."

"It's a good book, don't let me sway you otherwise. How about this, one day you'll read it on your own." He slipped it back on to the shelf.

"We'll see."

He took her hand in his. "So, you're falling for me?"

She laughed at his question. "As much as I would like to say no, there is a small part of me that might find you rather intriguing."

He leaned close to her, and for a moment Ally thought he might kiss her. A chill ran up her spine and her heart began to beat so fast she could swear her chest was moving up and down with the rhythm. Luke must have heard it as well, because a sly smile fell over his face.

"I want to show you something." He stepped away from her and moved over to the other side of the room. He approached a small black box that was set up on a shelf, and pressed a few buttons on it.

A loud sound immediately filled the room. Music. It was much different than the sounds that came out of the piano. Even back in the settlement they had a few old instruments that some of the older Ordinarys would play during the feasts. But this music was a combination of instruments, and they were accompanied by voices.

"What is this?" She laughed, listening to the fast pace music coming from the box. The voice was shouting out words rather than singing.

"They called this rock and roll, I believe." Luke smiled and played with the box some more. "Ah, here we go."

The music that filled the room now was much more serene and beautiful, the instruments accompanied by a female voice. Ally could almost make out what sounded like a piano in the background, and she found herself closing her eyes.

"Now this... this is beautiful", she said.

"Yeah, it is," Luke responded.

When Ally opened her eyes Luke was standing inches from her, having moved across the room quickly and quietly.

"It is said that humans from the old world used to dance to music like this," he added.

"We dance back in the settlement sometimes, but never to music this slow." She looked up at his violet eyes and noticed that they shone brighter than usual.

"I'll show you." Luke placed a hand on her waist and raised the other up near her shoulder. "Give me your hand."

She raised her hand up to meet his, and mimicked him by placing her other hand on his waist. Slowly he began to move to the side, taking her with him. Ally stumbled at first, but soon fell into a rhythm, finding that his feet moved in a sort of pattern. She leaned her head against his chest while they moved, listening to the steady beat of his heart.

The song ended and he stepped back so that he could see her. "My mom taught me to dance like that."

Ally smiled and nodded, not sure what to say. The moment was more intimate than any she had ever experienced, and it appeared as though Luke felt the same. They watched each other for a long moment before Luke made a move forward, his lips pausing inches from hers.

Ally had only ever kissed one boy, and it had been a dare from her friends. She had run up to him in the gathering hall at the settlement, planted a big, wet kiss on his lips, and ran away giggling. She had been ten, and she was pretty sure it didn't even count. To this day that boy still denied she ever touched him, especially around his girlfriend. She smiled at the thought.

"Does that smile mean that you're not going to slap me?" He hovered in front of her, his forehead leaning against her own.

"No, I think you're safe."

This time he moved all the way in and pressed his lips to hers. She found herself pushed up against one of the bookshelves and Luke's hands came up to cradle her face. This was nothing like the kiss she shared with the boy in her settlement when she was ten. Luke had probably kissed dozens of girls for practice. His lips moved expertly over hers, and soon she found a cadence to follow along with. She brought her hands up to the back of his neck, running her fingers over his thick hair. It had begun to grow out and she could almost hold onto it.

Ally had always thought that kissing a boy would be awkward, and that she would feel nervous and embarrassed afterward, but once Luke pulled away all she wanted to do was stare at him. She might have pulled him in for more kissing if Sabine hadn't showed up in the doorway and cleared her throat.

Luke didn't take his eyes off Ally. "Yes?"

Sabine tried to contain her smile. "Mazzi has dinner ready Mr. Lukin. Mr. and Mrs. Mathias will be dining with friends tonight. Would you like your dinner in your room, or would you like to dine in the kitchen with us?"

"Ally and I will be eating dinner in my room." He turned to look at her. "And Sabine, please call me Luke. Also, from now on, don't wait for me to address you before you feel like you can speak."

Sabine nodded and skipped from the room.

"Making some changes?" Ally's lip still tingled from the kiss.

"Some long overdo changes."

If only Stosh could see her now. He was on her mind often,

especially during her free time at the ORC, when all she could do was think. She wondered how he would react to all this new information if he had been here. How would he have handled learning about the ORC? He definitely wouldn't have expected her to be in a relationship. But she was about to dive head first into a romance with Luke Mathias, an Exceptional, and she was more than willing to take the plunge.

Chapter Thirteen

The next morning Ally woke up in Luke's bed, her arms stretched over her head. Last night they had eaten dinner and watched a movie from his collection that she had never seen. Somewhere in the middle of the story, she had gotten caught up in kissing Luke and missed crucial parts of the movie. The rest of the movie held a similar pattern and she didn't mind one bit. At some point she had fallen asleep in his arms, and he must have moved her to his bed. She sat up, smoothing down her unruly hair, and found that he was spread out on the couch across the room. He was asleep on his back, and one of his arms hung over the side of the couch.

"Such a gentleman," she mumbled, kicking her feet over the side of the bed and standing up.

Last night he mentioned that there was a good chance his father would still force him to uphold the contract set in place by the ORC, which meant that they had just a few short years to conceive a child or Luke would be required to choose another Ordinary. Ally didn't like the thought of him being with another girl, but she also didn't like the thought of being forced into that type of relationship with Luke. She wanted it to happen naturally, and in their own time, not on someone else's.

She tip toed across the room and opened the door as slowly as possible; thankful the doors in Luke's house didn't seem to creak. Back in the settlement, just turning the doorknob would have been enough to make her mother stir. She slipped into the hall and down to her room, glad to find that Sabine was awake and moving around. She must have recently returned from the shower because her long, red hair was leaving wet patches along the back of her grey shirt.

"Where were you last night?" Sabine teased.

"Your tone implies that I've been doing something bad." Ally smirked at her and pulled a fresh pair of clothes from her drawer.

Sabine giggled. "I think what you are doing is wonderful. It's about time you noticed Luke's advances toward you."

"We are just taking it slow." Ally said as she threw her dirty clothes into the hamper and pulled on the fresh ones. "It is a really strange situation."

Sabine rolled onto her stomach on her bed and rested her head in her hands. "A lot of Exceptionals fall for Ordinarys in the City. It isn't the majority, but there are dozens of married pairs."

Ally nodded. "I know, I'm just still not completely okay with what goes on here in the City. It seems odd to think about a future with the one Exceptional who is being groomed to one day run it."

"Maybe he'll change things. The ORC didn't even exist until Aden came into power. Maybe once he is gone, it will go away."

"We can only hope," Ally said quietly. "Hey, Luke mentioned taking me to see the Lake today. Do you know where that is?"

Sabine jumped onto her knees. "Oh, it's wonderful there. I've only been once. Mrs. Mathias wanted to go and took me along to carry her bags and serve her lunch. It is on the opposite end of the City, through the factories on the other end. Back before the virus it used to be a huge lake that stretched over a hundred miles wide. People used to swim in it and ride boats across it."

"Really?" Ally asked. She had seen these boats in one of the movies in Luke's room, and it was hard to imagine there being a place close by in which they used to exist.

"The Exceptionals didn't think it was necessary to take care of it like the old world humans did, so the lake has become uninhabitable. You'll see it for yourself. I'm sure Luke will fill you in." She crawled off the bed and grabbed her work list off her nightstand. "Have a fun day!"

By the time Ally got down to breakfast, Luke was already seated at the table with the others. Somehow he managed to wake up and put himself together faster than it took her just to change. Stosh always had the same tendencies, and he said it was one of the gifts of being a guy.

They ate breakfast quickly, and Ally barely spoke because all she could focus on was finishing and leaving with Luke. It was a Sunday so he didn't have any lessons or training sessions. It was also the first Sunday that they were able to spend together, since her previous ones in the City had been spent in the ORC.

When they stepped out of the house, Luke turned to her and smiled. "Remember when you first arrived, I told you about bikes?"

Ally thought for a minute. "I think so. You said it was another way to get around the City besides walking."

"Well, we are going to need to use one to get to the Lake. It would take up to two hours to walk there." He took her hand and pulled her down the walk.

At the end sat a small, silver vehicle. "This is a bike?"

"A version of one", he said as he ran his hand along the side of it. "Some require you to use your legs to pedal the bike forward, while others are powered on their own by either electricity or some sort of fuel. Since fuel is in such short supply, and saved for important necessities, this bike runs off electricity."

"How does that work?" Ally looked it over, thinking it didn't look sturdy enough to be carrying two people.

"There is a cord I use to plug it into an outlet in the garage," he answered. "The battery will last for six hours, so we will have plenty of time to travel to and from the Lake."

He stepped up to the bike and swung his leg over, positioning his hands on bars that stuck out on either side of the bike.

"Is it safe?" Ally approached the bike tentatively.

Luke smiled. "Pretty safe. Plus, I don't plan on letting anything happen to you."

She mimicked the way in which he had gotten on the bike, and settled in behind him.

"Hold on tight," he said, pressing the button that started the bike.

It rumbled to life beneath her and she quickly wrapped her arm around Luke's waist. The back of the bike sat much higher than the front so if she stretched, she was able to rest her chin on his shoulder and watch where they were going. She held on to him tightly, enjoying the way her body felt pressed up against his. This was one trip she wouldn't mind taking awhile.

THE BIKE MOVED QUICKLY through the streets but not fast enough that Ally felt afraid. The Exceptionals and Ordinarys moved out of their way, and soon they were zipping through the City Center and into the factory district. As they rode on, Luke explained over his shoulder that this was where many of the foods, lumber, and textiles were produced once supplies came in from the settlements. There was also an electric factory and a waste disposal building here. Ally thought the buildings looked old and dirty, but they were one of the main reasons the City had functioned as well as it had.

It took them thirty minutes to drive the bike to the Lake. When they arrived and Luke stopped the bike, Ally hopped off and ran to the edge of a concrete walk. It circled around the Lake, and there were signs that a short wall of some sort used to rise around it as well. Concrete rubble was strewn about in both large and small chunks.

"Amazing," was the first descriptive word that came out of her mouth.

Luke laced his fingers through hers and looked out over the Lake. "It's intriguing, isn't it?"

"Sabine said that in the old world, boats used to drive on it and people would swim in it. She said it was big, but I don't think I realized just *how* big."

The Lake stretched as far out as she could see. To her right she could see one of the City boundary walls jutting out into the water. It went out about twenty yards before cutting off completely. She looked to the left but couldn't see the boundary wall on that side, which meant it was some distance away.

"I wonder what is on the other side."

"More Wilderness," Luke answered. "There is no way to cross the water anymore."

Ally had seen lakes and large bodies of water in some of the movies they had watched, and this Lake bore no resemblance to them. Green weeds grew in tangled knots along the shore, and the water closest to them sat stagnant with green moss on top. Further out, she could see some water moving against the blanket of green, but just barely. For a brief moment the moss reminded her of Stosh. It was the same color as his eyes, and her own.

"What happened to it?" she asked.

Luke shrugged. "The first generation of Exceptionals didn't find it a priority for care when they were getting the City back in order. Humans in the old world used to fish out of it, which was another source of food we could have used, but the maintenance was too time consuming. Eventually, it began to look like this, so technically it is now more of a marsh than a lake."

"Thanks for bringing me," she said. "It is like nothing I've ever seen."

"I think everyone needs to see it at least once," he said as turned away from the water. "Come on, I want to show you something over here."

He led her down the concrete path and to a small, stone building that overlooked the Lake. It had a shape similar to that of a house, except it was much smaller and the walls were open to the elements. A stone pole in either corner held up the pointed roof. When they stepped inside, Ally found that someone had set up blankets and pillows along the floor, and there was even a couch and a small table pushed into the corner.

"What is this place?" she asked as she leaned against one of the weathered, stone poles.

"It used to be a pavilion. Families would come here to eat and hang out while they were resting from their day out on the lake. There are others scattered around the shore, and they are not all in such great shape." He dropped her hand and plopped down on the blankets, looking up at her.

She sat down next to him and wrapped her arms around her

knees. "Sometimes, when I was younger, I would close my eyes and try to imagine the people who lived in our home in the settlement before we did. I tried to imagine what they might look like and dress like, and what jobs they went to each day. I tried to imagine a time when there were no Exceptionals and Ordinarys and just human beings. Everyone working together equally."

She heard Luke take a deep breath beside her. "Humans from the old world didn't always work together or live as equals. There were debates, and feuds, and many wars. Even then there were classes of people. Did you know that some families lived on the street, with no homes at all? They slept under bridges and begged for food on the corners in the City."

"That is hard to believe." Ally looked over at him. "Where did you hear that?"

"Our history courses at the Institute touch on it sometimes. The old world humans weren't as great as some people make them out to be. We may have problems, but they had their own as well."

When Ally imagined the world that existed before the virus, she had always glamorized the lives of the people who lived in it. She had assumed that people were happier and more fulfilled. They could do anything and go anywhere, not having to worry about Exceptionals ruling over them. She couldn't imagine that they had hardships like the Ordinarys faced in the settlement. But as Luke spoke to her, she realized just how naïve her view was.

"Do you think if we had been born two hundred years ago, before the virus, that we would have found our way to each other?" She took a hold of his hand, running her finger over his.

"I think there is a good possibility. What if I hadn't left the City and gone to the creek the day I had met you? What if you hadn't jumped the creek and were able to return to your settlement that night? I can think of a dozens things that could have been done differently to affect our meeting, yet here we are. I don't know what the future holds for us, but I think it is going to be something great. The circumstances of the time we live in is what brought us together, but maybe something similar would have happened in the past. Either way, I'd like to think our lives are intertwined." He squeezed her hand.

She lay back onto the blanket and closed her eyes, trying to picture the Lake as it had once been. She could almost picture the moss-free water and the people, their skin tanned from playing in the sun all day. "I bet a lot of memories were made on this lake."

She felt Luke lay down beside her and he slipped his arm over her waist. "Lots of memories have been made since."

Ally opened her eyes and looked up at him. "I'm betting many were made right here in this building."

He laughed and leaned back on the blanket. "I guess you could say that."

She rolled onto her side and propped herself up on her elbow. "How many memories have *you* made here, Luke?"

She kept her voice light, but it had been something she had been curious about. He rolled onto his side so that their bodies leaned into each other, and their lips were practically touching.

"You would be my first," he said with a smile, kissing her gently on the lips.

Ally wasn't sure if she would ever get used to Luke kissing her, and the feeling that coursed through her body when he did. She wasn't even sure if she wanted to get used to it. She couldn't imagine no longer feeling the thrill that ran through her veins when their lips met.

"Not today." She smiled, looking into his violet eyes. "But you are more than welcome to kiss me as much as you want."

"I think I can handle that." He pushed her backward onto the blanket, moving the top half of his body over hers. His lips pressed to hers gently at first, and then with more eagerness.

He pulled back after a few minutes. "But seriously, Ally. There has never been anyone before you, and I can't imagine anyone after you. I've never been caught up in dating or kissing girls for the fun of it. The Exceptional girls here could never compare to you."

Ally smiled up at him and her insides felt like they might burst. She had never imagined that such a good feeling could exist. She had never even believed that she could ever feel this way about a boy. She didn't want to become one of those girls that followed the boys around like a duckling followed its mother. She only depended on herself. Now, Luke was starting to change her whole view on the subject. And as he leaned down to her and pressed his lips to her neck, she could finally see why love might be something worth having a desire for.

They lay in the pavilion for another hour or so before finally hopping back on the bike. For the ride home Ally rested her cheek against Luke's back and closed her eyes, letting the wind whip around her body. Being with Luke made her feel alive, more alive than she ever imagined she would feel in the City. Back in the ORC, she thought she would never feel whole again unless she could be back in the settlement with her family. She thought that she needed her old life and friends back in order to find herself again. But she had been wrong; she could feel all of that here with Luke. Maybe living in the City for the remainder of her life wouldn't be such a bad thing after all.

Chapter Fourteen

It had been almost a week since Luke had brought Ally home from the ORC. If someone had asked him then if he thought that he and Ally would be together right now, spending all of their free time with each other, he would have laughed in their face. He thought that she would still be broken from her time in the ORC, still mad at him for not telling her about it before she was sent there. Sometimes he still expected her to wake up in the morning and dislike him all over again.

But she didn't, at least not yet.

Every morning she woke up in his bed. He would hold her in his arms until she fell asleep and then he would slip onto the couch, giving her the space she needed. He knew that one day their relationship would progress further, but right now it needed time to grow and develop.

Sometimes he would hear her mumbling in her sleep.

"Stosh" and "Willow" were the names mentioned most frequently, and it pained him to think about how much she missed her family and friends. Willow was in the City, so there was hope that one day they would be reunited, but the same couldn't be said for Ally and her brother.

It was Saturday and Ally had already made plans to spend the morning running errands with Sabine. He and Ally had spent so much time together lately that she hadn't been able to be with the other Ordinarys in the house. He was the one who suggested they take some time apart today. It would be a good idea if he spent some time with Pax and Maver as well.

He dressed and slipped out of the house, walking to Pax's house on autopilot. If the streets had been made of dirt, he imagined that he would have worn his own path in by now. Pax and Maver were waiting for him in Pax's bedroom, which was quite similar to his own.

"I want to go over the wall today," he said as soon as he entered the room.

"You're joking, right?" Maver laughed.

"No. I need to go to Ally's settlement", he responded.

Pax rolled his eyes. "I thought we were going to have non-Ally time today."

"She isn't here, is she?" Luke motioned around him. "Plus, I overheard my father in his office a few days ago. They are increasing security around the boundary line in a week's time. They even have plans to put a sensor line along the top of the boundary wall. Ordinarys of course cannot scale the wall, and have never tried, but someone reported that Exceptionals were sneaking out of the City and into the woods."

Maver laughed. "We're famous."

"Let's make one last run through the woods while we can," Luke said. He added excitement to his voice, hoping it might help convince them.

Pax groaned. "I graduate from Guard training in two days. If I get caught, they might never let me move on."

"Consider this one last hurrah before you are required to rat us out." Maver slapped Pax on the back.

"Fine." Pax stood. "But let's be quick about it."

THIRTY MINUTES LATER they stood at the bottom of the boundary wall. It was the same spot they used each time they chose to leave the city. Since the wall here curved into a deep arc, and the town homes came close to touching it, it was hard for the patrol Guards to spot anyone who might be trying to climb it. Luke scaled the wall first, using the strength in his arms to climb to the top.

"You know," Pax said as he pulled himself up onto the wall next. "You could have easily used your abilities to bring yourself, and the rest of us, up here."

"We've done it with out them before." Luke grinned. "I like a challenge."

Pax shook his head, and Luke could sense some tension between them. He knew that Pax and Maver had been bothered by the fact that he hadn't told them about his extra abilities, but he knew they would grow to understand. He didn't want anyone else to have the burden of keeping that secret. Its discovery had brought enough harm to Ally, and he knew others would have suffered as well had they known.

Maver appeared over the top of the wall next, pulling himself up with a grunt. "I wouldn't mind some of those special abilities right about now."

Maver was one of the few Exceptionals in the City that had been born with no abilities. It was a rarity, and many of these Exceptionals were looked down on. Sometimes they were sent to work in the factories with the Ordinarys and stripped of their Exceptional rights, but not Maver. He had managed to escape that fate, and Luke sometimes wondered if it was because they were friends. Having Aden as a father wasn't always a bad thing. His father was happy to surround himself, and his family, with those weaker than them.

140

They scaled down the opposite side and landed in the soft underbrush below. This was the same path they had taken when they had been in the woods almost a month ago. The same day that they had run into Ally and her brother.

"Which way?" Maver asked.

Luke pulled a small map from his pocket. He had taken it from his father's office that morning, knowing he could return it before Aden even knew that it was missing. He unfolded it carefully, and the others stepped over to take a look. The map showed the City and the wall around it. Dotted in the outskirts was each settlement, represented by the marking the Ordinarys there wore on their forearms.

He placed his finger on the one marked Oakwood. "This is where Ally is from. It isn't too far from here."

"What exactly are we looking for there?" Pax asked.

"I need to find Ally's brother. I want her family to know that she is okay," Luke answered.

Pax raised his eyebrow. "You really care about her, don't you?"

"More than you know," Luke said, shoving the map back into his pocket. He took off at a run into the woods.

At their Exceptional speed, they crossed over the creek and into Ordinary territory in just five minutes. It was another ten minutes before they came upon signs that they were drawing close to a settlement. They slowed their pace and stepped through the woods carefully, trying to make as little noise as possible. Soon, old homes loomed up in front of them, many of them falling apart and obviously uninhabited.

"Ally mentioned that her brother is a woodcutter, so he'll probably be out working. I'll need you to take care of the others, Pax, so that I can talk to him." Luke stopped at a tree and turned to face his friends.

Pax smirked. "I knew there was a reason you brought me along."

Pax had one ability that Luke knew of and it was the ability to put people to sleep with just his touch. Depending on how long he touched them, they could be out anywhere from five minutes to five days. It was one of the main reasons he had been chosen to train for the Guard. His ability would come in use often in his future line of work.

"I also brought you because you're always up for an adventure." Luke gave him a light punch to the shoulder and started through the woods again.

They circled around the backs of the houses, coming up on a nicer section of homes. These homes had small vegetable gardens in the back, and looked more maintained. Several children ran through the dirt streets squealing in delight, and several female Ordinarys carried large baskets of laundry nearby. They all wore matching black outfits. He concentrated on their arms, trying to catch a glimpse of their markings. One of the women raised her arm to wipe the sweat from her brow, and when she did her shirtsleeve slid up, revealing the Oak tree on her forearm. They were definitely in the right settlement.

"Look at this place," Maver whispered. "All of these Ordinarys."

They had never gone far enough into the woods to see a settlement. It had never really interested them before, but now all three of them found it mesmerizing. The homes all circled around each other into a miniature community, and the Ordinarys moved about with such freedom. For a moment, Luke wondered what it would be like to live with out the expectations and rules of his father. What would it be like to

142

not have to attend lessons or training sessions, and to spend his days exploring the woods and working the land?

"Luke, we should move along," Pax said, pointing out that the women with the laundry were headed in their direction.

They slipped further west from the City and to what appeared to be the edge of this settlement. Finally they came upon the large warehouse that seemed to serve as lumber production for the City. At least a dozen males were outside the building, either chopping wood down or helping to transport it inside.

"That's him." Luke picked Stosh out immediately. He stood next to an Ordinary much older than him, and the two of them were pointing at something on the warehouse roof.

"Are you sure?" Maver asked.

Luke nodded. "Don't you recognize him from the creek? Plus, his features are just like Ally's, and they're twins."

"Whoa," Pax said. "I didn't know that."

Twins were another rarity in the City. Luke hadn't seen any born in his lifetime, and he wasn't sure if his father had either.

"Pax. You're on." Luke gave him a small push.

Pax strolled out into the open, drawing attention to himself almost immediately. He was wearing muted gray Ordinary clothes that they kept hidden for when they wanted to leave the City, but since the Ordinarys here wore black, it wasn't much of a disguise. It was his violet eyes, tremendous height, and buzzed head that gave him away as an Exceptional. Most of the men had hair that hung to their eyes, and a few even had their hair in low ponytails at their necks. The Ordinarys seemed confused at first, and then grew leery as Pax came closer.

Pax raised his hands in the air. "No need to worry. I'm here with a message from the City."

Stosh and the older man shared a skeptical look, but gathered around Pax like the others. Luke wondered if Stosh would recognize Pax from the boundary line, but it didn't seem like he did. In one extremely fast motion, Pax swept his arm around, striking half of them at once. The Ordinarys he touched immediately crumpled to the ground and remained still. He grabbed hold of the remaining Ordinarys, with the exception of Stosh, and had them all asleep in seconds.

Luke and Maver stepped out from behind the trees and strolled toward the pile of bodies. Stosh crossed his arms over his chest and stood up taller than he had been, his head held high.

"I knew I recognized you. What did you do to them?" He motioned to his co-workers.

Pax shrugged. "They are just taking a little nap."

When Luke and Maver reached Pax's side, Stosh looked the three of them over.

Luke motioned for Pax and Maver to step back. "I'm here about Ally."

Stosh's guard dropped slightly when Luke mentioned his sister's name. "What about her?"

"I need you to know that she is safe. I need you to tell your mother this as well, but do not tell anyone that we came to see you," Luke said.

Stosh laughed and looked at the men piled up around his feet. "I think it will be a bit obvious."

Luke shook his head. "They'll wake up in just a minute, and they won't even remember what happened. By the time they are up and moving, they'll believe that they had been working the whole time."

144

Stosh's mouth hung open for a moment. "How do I know Ally is safe?"

"I can only give you my word," he responded. "She needed you to know."

"Did she send you?" Stosh's brows furrowed together.

"Not exactly," Luke said carefully.

"What have you done with her?" He said through gritted teeth, taking a step toward Luke.

Luke raised his hands. "I haven't hurt her, if that is what you are implying. Like I told you, she is safe and doing just fine."

Stosh narrowed his eyes. "I don't believe that she is fine. This isn't what she wanted. Tell her that the only place she'll be safe is home with her family."

With that he spun on his heels and stalked toward the warehouse, disappearing through the large doors that led inside.

At Luke's feet, one of the men groaned and his eyes began to flutter. Pax leaned forward and grabbed Luke's arm. "We have to go."

Luke took one last look at the Warehouse Stosh had disappeared within. Ally's brother had been right. She wasn't *just fine*, she was getting by; making the most of what she had been given in the City. He tried to ignore Stosh's comments, but they weighed heavily on his mind. He raced Pax and Maver back to the wall, the three of them touching the stones almost at the exact same time.

"Foot races just aren't the same in the City," Maver laughed, starting to pull himself up the wall.

"I couldn't agree more," Luke responded, following his lead.

Once they were over the wall and into the City, they retrieved a bag they had hidden in a bush nearby. They pulled clean, white uniforms from it and changed behind one of the homes, throwing the gray clothes into a nearby trash bin. They slipped into the street and made their way toward the City Center, falling into the foot traffic of the other Exceptionals.

"Did you accomplish what you went out there for?" Maver whispered beside Luke.

He nodded. "I did what I could."

Pax spotted a few of his fellow Guard trainees and took off from the group, saying that maybe he would see them at the Warehouse tomorrow, the biggest fight day of the month. They ran into a group of friends from the Institute who happened to be going to the Warehouse this afternoon. Maver joined them but Luke decided against going, choosing to head home to Ally instead. She would be back from her errands with Sabine soon and all he wanted to do right now was spend more time with her.

On the way to his house, he battled with whether or not he would tell her about his trip to see Stosh. If she knew that Luke could leave the City so easily, she might ask him to take her to see her family, or even to help her escape. He knew that she cared for him, and wanted to be with him, but the temptation might be too much. If he didn't tell her, it might backfire on him like the ORC had. In the end, he decided to wait until she brought the subject of her family or the settlement up again before he would determine what he would do.

Chapter Fifteen

The following morning, Ally slipped out of Luke's bed and walked over to where he lay sleeping on the couch. With a smile on her face, she leaned forward and jumped onto his chest, holding her head up so that she could see his expression. Instead of being entertained by the sight of his surprised face, she learned the lesson that you should never surprise an Exceptional. Especially one with strong abilities.

Luke's violet eyes popped open and she was shot up into the air. Before gravity could bring her back down, she found herself floating just inches from the ceiling. Luke still lay on the couch below her, his palms facing up at her.

"Not a good idea." Luke's face held a stern expression but as he continued to look at her, it softened until his mouth pulled up in a crooked smile. "I like having this kind of power over you."

Once Ally's body had landed safely on his, she leaned forward and kissed him quickly. "Sorry about that. I guess I didn't expect that much of a reaction from you."

Luke laughed. "I've never had someone sneak up on me before."

"No way." She gave him a look of disbelief. "Stosh and I had a running tally going of how many times we could scare each other. I was just starting to pull ahead before I left the settlement."

Ally noticed Luke's expression change at the mention of her

147

brother. He seemed to be struggling privately, as if he had something he needed to say.

"Luke?" She said reached out and touched his face.

Rather than responding, he grabbed the back of her head and pulled her in for a kiss. A moment later he had her flipped underneath pressed his body into hers, his lips grazing her neck ever so softly.

A small moan escaped her throat before she pushed him back. "You make it hard for me to hold myself back."

He kissed her hard on the mouth before pushing himself up and off of her, leaning back against the couch. "That isn't such a bad thing."

She cocked her head, shooting him a look, and rolled off the couch. "What's the plan for today?"

"I was actually thinking about going to the Warehouse today. It's the first Sunday of the month, which is the biggest fight day." He grabbed hold of her and pulled her down on his lap.

She wrapped her arms around his neck and looked up at him. "Oh, could I come with you? I'm interested in seeing what that place is all about."

Luke frowned. "I wish you could, but it would be a very bad idea. Besides, I doubt you would enjoy it as much as you think."

"Why not?" She said, implying that the question was for both parts of what he had said.

He used a free hand to tuck a strand of her hair behind her ear. "The Warehouse rules change on the first Sunday of the month. It is the day when Exceptionals can bring things to barter with in their fights, including Ordinarys. If you came, another Exceptional could challenge me to a fight and demand that I hand over my contract with you if I lose."

"Couldn't you just refuse?" Ally understood why Luke had said she wouldn't enjoy the Warehouse very much. It was just another place for Ordinarys to be objectified and mistreated.

"I could refuse to fight, but that really isn't my style. And even if I knew I could win, it wouldn't be worth the risk. It is much easier to leave you here, where I know you'll be safe."

Ally smiled. "I guess I can understand that. I'm sure Sabine has more errands that I can run with her."

"That's another thing." Luke gave her a push off his lap and stood up beside her. "I need you to stay home today, just in case. Sundays are big at the Warehouse, and I don't want to risk something happening to you while I'm there, or because I'm there."

She nodded her head, even though inwardly she could feel the rebellious side of her fighting to speak up. She didn't want to be controlled, or treated weaker than anyone else, but there were still many things she didn't understand about the City.

"Maybe I'll spend some time in the garden today. I haven't been to the fountain in awhile," she thought out loud.

"I'm glad someone is enjoying that place as much as my mother used to." He pulled away from her and slipped into the bathroom to get ready.

Ally ended up spending the morning folding laundry with Sabine, and helping Mazzi rearrange the kitchen cabinets. Even though they were not her chores, she felt like she had a purpose by helping. She didn't want the other Ordinarys to think of her just as Luke's ORC contract. She wanted to be worth more.

After they had eaten a light lunch Sabine checked her work list. "I have to run some errands to the outer suburbs. Do you want to come with?"

Ally hesitated, thinking back to what Luke had said earlier. Maybe he had just assumed that Sabine and Ally couldn't handle themselves outside of the home if something were to happen. She didn't want to stay inside every time Luke went to the Warehouse with his friends, or to the Institute.

"Only if Asher comes," she said, coming up with some sort of compromise in her head.

Asher looked up from his lunch, seeming surprised that Ally had asked him to come along. "Um, okay."

By the time they left the house and were on their way toward the outer suburbs, Ally already felt better about her decision. She was walking between Sabine and Asher and she took a moment to loop each of her arms through one of theirs.

"I could stay out in this warm weather all day long. I don't want the summer to end," Ally said.

They were in the third month of summer, which was generally the hottest, but it also meant that chillier weather was right around the corner.

"You've seemed... happy, lately." Asher said, his arm tense under hers.

"I have been happy. I *am* happy," she responded. "What do you expect me to feel?"

Sabine shrugged. "We are glad you are happy, Ally. It is just concerning how quickly you flipped a switch between being emotionally broken in the ORC to being bright and chipper back home. It is what I wanted for you, especially with how comfortable you've become with Luke, but do you think maybe you're pushing your other feelings aside

150

and not dealing with them?"

Ally pulled her arms from theirs and wrapped them over her stomach. "I can't sit around and focus on the negative anymore. My situation isn't going to change, so I need to make what I can of it. Plus, I have Luke now. If I need to be in the City for the rest of my life, with him is where I want to be. One day, when Luke is leader, we'll get the ORC shut down and then I'll really be able to let those memories go."

"I just hope that he lives up to everything you believe him to be." Asher said in a low voice.

"Me too," Ally said, focusing on the street in front of her.

"So, where are we headed?" Asher changed the subject.

"Mrs. Mathias needs me to pick up a message from an acquaintance of hers. Apparently they don't currently have an Ordinary that can deliver it. Then we need to stop at the market and get more fruits and vegetables. Pretty simple." Sabine took another look at her list before folding it neatly and placing it back in her pocket.

"Exceptionals can be so lazy sometimes." Asher rolled his eyes. "Sure, they say that they are busy training and taking lessons, but the majority of them that have already graduated waste their time on stupid activities."

Ally had never heard Asher speak like this before. He always completed his work list each day with out complaint.

"You would like it in the settlement." She turned her head so that she could look at him.

"You think?" he asked.

"No person there is more important than another. Sure, some jobs may seem harder than others, but we are always reminded that even the small pieces of the puzzle hold us all together." Ally thought back to all the times she had heard Po give the same speech to a younger Ordinary that wasn't completely happy with his or her work assignment.

"And when it isn't a work day, we can run through the woods, swim in the ponds, and do whatever we want. The Guards only patrol through two or three times a week, so for the most part it is Exceptional free. There may not be as many luxuries there, running water for one, but the settlement definitely has its positives."

As Ally spoke to Asher, she could feel a longing growing within her. From the moment she walked through the stone tunnel into the City, a part of her started to consider that she would forever be stuck within these walls. Ordinarys had never returned home before, so why would she? Then once she was in the ORC it became clear why no one came home. They were not allowed. Since then she had come to an understanding with herself that she would live in the City with Luke, and that they would be happy together. But what if she could go back to the settlement? What if she were given the choice? Would she choose to go home and be with her family, or would she choose to stay here with Luke?

"Ally…" Sabine grabbed her arm.

"Sorry, my mind was wandering again," she responded. Ally was sure that they were wondering why she had suddenly stopped talking to them.

"No, Ally." Sabine pointed in front of them.

They had reached the outer suburbs, the area of the City with smaller homes that were all shoved together tightly along the main road. Despite the volume of homes, there were barely any Exceptionals or Ordinarys on the street. Either they were in the City Center at this time of day, or they were inside their homes relaxing.

Ally followed Sabine's finger to a spot in the road about twenty yards in front of them. Four Exceptionals stood there, spread out across the width of the street. There were three males and one female, and one of the males stood out further from the rest. Ally figured he must be the leader of their little group because he looked like he was trying awfully hard to be a tough guy.

"Tighe," Asher said under his breath before turning to Ally and Sabine. "We should get out of here."

The name sounded familiar to Ally, but she couldn't quite place it. The Exceptionals moved forward, their quick steps covering the short distance in seconds. Now they stood just a yard in front of Ally, Sabine, and Asher, their violet eyes narrowing in a threatening way.

"Can you let us pass?" Ally asked, trying to make it obvious how unimpressed she was with the four Exceptionals.

The male in front, the one Asher had addressed as Tighe, smirked. "Normally I would. But today... today I have plans for you, Ally."

Ally shivered at the way he said her name. "What would those plans be?"

"You are just going to have to come along and find out," he said as he stepped toward her.

What happened next was a blur to Ally, but from what she could gather, Asher tried to step in front of her in some sort of defense. Either with abilities or the use of his Exceptional strength, Tighe sent Asher flying across the road and into some trash bins outside one of the homes.

Ally put her hands up. "I'll go with you, you don't need to hurt my friends."

"Maybe they should be more careful," Tighe spat at Sabine.

153

Sabine squealed and backed up, cowering behind Ally.

"Sabine, go see if Asher is okay. Then I want you take him home," Ally said, hoping that once home, Sabine could find Luke and tell him what had happened.

Sabine nodded quickly and rushed to the side of the road, leaning over Asher's body. The collision had knocked him out, but since Sabine managed to remain calm, Ally determined that he must at least still be alive.

"This is Luke's Ordinary? Are you sure?" The female Exceptional sneered. She had long dark hair pulled into a slick, high ponytail. She was tall, like the others, and had angular cheekbones that jutted out of her already intense face.

"I'm sure. We better go before a crowd begins to gather," Tighe said.

Ally noticed that a few Exceptionals had stopped to watch them. They didn't seem overly worried about her well-being, or about Asher's limp body on the ground. They probably witnessed this type of Ordinary treatment every day. Tighe grabbed a hold of Ally's arm and began to pull her along, keeping his grip tight. The four of them didn't share any conversation as she was pulled through the streets. She doubted the Exceptionals had much to say to each other that she was welcome to hear.

They walked past homes and shops, and even right past Luke's neighborhood. She hoped that Asher was starting to come to and that Sabine could get him on his feet and home soon. Flint could easily find Luke, or even Pax and Maver, and explain what had happened. Ally tried not to focus on how mad Luke would be when he found out she had left the house, but instead how relieved he would be to get her back

154

safely. She just needed to figure out where Tighe was taking her, and hoped that Luke would as well. Suddenly, she knew where she had heard his name before.

"I recognize your name now," she said. "You are the Exceptional who always challenges Luke to fights. Hasn't he beaten you several times?"

Tighe stopped in his tracks and jerked her body around to face him. "If I were you, I would keep my mouth shut. Hasn't anyone taught you that Ordinarys don't speak unless spoken to?"

Ally made a show of biting down on her lips. She really shouldn't have spoken at all, but the realization of who Tighe was gave her a better idea of where he was taking her. As they drew closer to the City Center, her suspicions were confirmed. Flint wouldn't need to find Luke; Tighe would be taking Ally right to him.

Luke had told her just this morning that he needed her to stay home for her own safety, that today was a bad day for her to be out unprotected. She should have listened to him, but it was too late to change that now, no matter how much she wished she could reverse time. Tighe apparently had big plans for today, and they included challenging Luke to a fight. This time, he would have Ally to barter with, and Luke would have to either oblige him or forfeit his contract with her.

"What have I done?" Ally mumbled, realizing that she might have given up everything good she had found in the City. Today she just might lose Luke.

Chapter Sixteen

The Warehouse loomed up in front of them. It was easy to pick out seeing as it was the oldest looking building in City Center. It reminded Ally of the factories they had passed on their way to the Lake. Luke had once explained that the Exceptional teens didn't want the maintenance crews to work on the appearance. They liked the run down look it had.

Two lines stretched in either direction in front of the building, and one of them was even starting to curve around the side. Tighe and his friends marched her right up to the double doors, where two teen Exceptionals stood. They were obviously training to become Guards by the way they stood at attention. She felt that familiar uneasiness in her gut as they looked down at her.

"Tighe," One of the Exceptionals nodded his head and leaned back, opening the door for them. Ally was shoved forward through the doors and into the crowded entryway of the building. Ally could immediately see that the Warehouse was one big open space. The upper floors had been cleared out to open up the building, making the ceiling visible several stories above. Bright lights lit the large room and as she was pushed further forward, she could see a make shift concrete circle to the right. It appeared to be a ring for the fights to take place in. In a building this size, she was sure there was more than one of these.

The crowd to her left cheered loudly, signaling that something exciting was happening in one of the current fights. Ally couldn't see much around her at the moment, since all of the Exceptionals were much taller than her. Tighe regained a hold on her arm and pulled her forward, using his free arm to push Exceptionals out of their way.

"Find Luke," Tighe said to the female Exceptional who had been traveling with them. She nodded and disappeared into the wall of bodies in front of them.

"He has been here all afternoon, he will probably be leaving soon," one of the males beside her said.

"Not with her here he won't," Tighe grinned.

They finally pushed their way out of the crowd and into the middle of the room. Ally took the chance to grab a better look around, finding that she was right about there being multiple places to fight. There were two rings on either side of the area they stood in now, and each area was surrounded by rows of seats that staggered upward at least one story. It appeared to be built that way so that everyone in the crowd could have a view. The ring closest to her on the left, where the cheers had come from, was now empty and being prepped for a new fight. Ordinarys swept the floor, mopping up bodily fluids that Ally couldn't identify. She suddenly felt nauseous.

Where they stood now, there were two tables set up with an Exceptional seated at each. A line of Exceptionals formed on either side, waiting to sign up for a fight. As they approached the table one by one, the Exceptional seated there would ask them a few questions and punch information into the porta-comp.

A familiar voice filled the space behind her. "What's this Tighe, you've come back for more? I've already beaten you three times this year. Are you sure you want to make it four?"

The ease in Luke's voice told her that he hadn't noticed her. She started to turn and felt Tighe hold her in place. One of his friends had stepped in front of her, blocking her from Luke's sight.

"Fourth time's a charm," Tighe responded. "And this time I'm bringing a deal to the table."

"I don't have anything on me," Luke responded. "Are you prepared to lose whatever *you* brought?"

Luke's voice sounded so cocky and confident. It was a side of him she had only seen once or twice since she had arrived in the City, and she wondered if he always acted this way when she was not around.

"Are you?" Tighe said.

At that moment his friend stepped out of the way and Tighe spun Ally around. Her eyes immediately met Luke's and she watched his poised demeanor fade for just a moment. He regained his composure and she watched as his jaw tightened, his violet eyes glowing with fury.

"No way," He spat. "She isn't yours to barter."

"Well, I found her wandering around in the outer suburbs of the City, not anywhere near your home, so I'd have to say that she is *mine*."

Ally didn't like being talked about as though she was a possession, and it was just a reminder that she would always be viewed as lesser than the others. Another Ordinary to be owned and passed around.

Luke's gaze flickered down to her. "Is this true?"

His tone was accusatory and the weight of his glare forced her to stare at the floor. She managed a nod and flinched as Luke cursed under his breath.

"So, as I see it, you have two options. Fight for her, or lose her." Tighe shrugged like it was no big deal.

"I'll do it," Luke growled, his hands clenched into fists at his side. Pax and Maver stood on either side of him, their expressions just as threatening.

Ally realized he didn't have much of a choice. Well, he could say no and leave her with Tighe, but he wouldn't do that. Not Luke.

A satisfied smile fell on Tighe's face and he pulled Ally over to the registration table, knocking another Exceptional out of the way. The person seated at the table, a younger female, opened her mouth to tell him off but then saw who was standing in front of her.

"Oh, Tighe. Opponent?" she asked, grabbing the porta-comp next to her.

"Luke." He grinned, not bothering to finish the name. They had obviously done this enough times to be considered regular competitors.

The girl paused for a second and then pressed the screen a few times. She handed him the porta-comp and he pressed a button on the screen. Luke stepped up beside her and took the porta-comp, touching his finger to the screen in the same way that Tighe had. He took a moment to glance at Ally, a somber look in his eyes, and then turned to rejoin Pax and Maver.

"We want Arena One," Tighe demanded.

The girl nodded. "The last fight in One just finished so they are clearing it out now. I'll send this e-comm to the Ref while you go prep."

Tighe began to pull Ally away but she struggled against him. "Can't I go with Luke? I'll sit with Maver and Pax during the fight."

"Yeah, right, and risk them running off with you," he shook his head.

"Isn't that against the rules?" She sneered.

"You'll be coming with us," he said as he pulled her roughly, forcing her through the crowd. Was Luke watching their interaction, or had he already gone to prep for the fight?

She was led along the back wall of the warehouse, passing the ring closest to the registration table. Two shirtless Exceptionals circled around the concrete slab, hands facing out. One's hands were pulsating with a bright, green light. He pushed his hands forward and the green light shot at his opponent. Ally was sure the other Exceptional was going to be blown to bits but instead he blinked and disappeared from sight, reappearing after the green beam had passed. She also noticed that there was some sort of invisible wall around the ring to prevent anything from happening to the crowd. It had flashed blue for a moment when the green beam hit it.

The crowd of Exceptionals pushed toward them, struggling to find a seat from which they could watch. This fight must be *the* fight to see today. The air pulsed around her, filling with the excitement of the crowd. The back of her neck tingled and she could almost feel their adrenaline coursing through her own body.

Tighe led her to Arena One and motioned for her to sit on a wooden bench just a few yards from the circular ring. After making sure his friends had secured a seat on either side of her, he pulled his shirt over his head and jumped around on his feet, stretching his arms above his head.

His top half was hardened with muscles and not a single ounce of fat jiggled as he moved. Ally couldn't take her eyes off him, still finding herself in awe of the strength the Exceptionals exhibited. Tighe turned and looked at her for a moment, a sly smile on his face.

"Like what you see?" He winked at her and she rolled her eyes.

He shrugged and stepped into the ring, continuing his odd, jumpy stretches. Across the room, Luke stepped into the ring, a determined look on his face. He was also shirtless, something Ally had

160

seen before, but the lights above the Arena created deep contrasts across his body. He looked larger and more menacing, and the sight made her insides light on fire.

Luke had been here for several hours. Ally wasn't sure exactly how many fights he had completed, but she could see that he wasn't at his best. His face already glistened with sweat and the glow in his eyes was dimming. A female Exceptional, most likely the Ref, stepped up to the Arena and pulled a lever beside it. A blue flash appeared around the circle, signaling the appearance of the invisible wall Ally had noticed in the neighboring ring. It also seemed to signal the start of the fight because Tighe and Luke began to slowly circle each other. Their hands faced outward, like Ally had seen the others do, and they kept their eyes focused on each other.

Tighe's hands began to glow with an orange light and Ally found herself bouncing her legs. She had no idea what his abilities were compared to Luke's, but she could at least find comfort in the fact that Luke had beaten Tighe at least three times before.

"Tighe has been training," the male to her right spoke. "He has been honing a new ability specifically for this."

Ally wasn't sure why he was talking to her. Maybe to make her nervous? If so, it worked. Especially as she watched Luke take in Tighe's glowing hands. He was obviously startled by the sight, and therefore had never seen it before. Had Tighe lost to Luke on purpose previously, just to have a final win? Had he planned on having Ally to barter with? She shuddered at the thought and brought her hands to her mouth, biting at her finger nails. Her mother always discouraged this habit, saying it was a particularly nasty one, but she wasn't here to give Ally disapproval.

The glowing in Tighe's hands burned bright until finally, and quicker than Ally could follow, he brought his hands together in front of him. A giant ball of fire shot forward toward Luke. Luke was fast, but the initial shock cost him a small burn to the side of his arm. Ally let out a worried gasp and the male to her right laughed.

"Told you," he said with a grin.

She elbowed him in the side, which probably hurt her more than it hurt him, but she felt some satisfaction in the action. He glared down at her, looking as if he might reciprocate, but then his gaze found its way back to the fight.

Luke was raising his hands up now, and in an instant Tighe was lifted off his feet, his body dangling in the air. He moved his hands to the right and Tighe's body was thrown into the side of the Arena, and then lifted into the air once again.

"Luke's been practicing too." Ally looked over at the same male and smirked.

"Tighe is still stronger. Their fights never last long, it should be over soon," he grunted.

She felt like they had barely started, but the Arena next to theirs had already cleared out even though that fight had just begun when they were walking over. If one Exceptional was stronger than the other, it could be easy to win in seconds. But Luke and Tighe seemed almost evenly matched, both exhibiting new abilities.

The Ref gave some sort of warning shout, a word Ally didn't hear, and Luke set Tighe back on the ground.

"There are rules against holding someone in the air for a long period of time. Luke could hold him there all night and there would never be any action," the male droned on. She wondered what the male

162

on her left was thinking. Did he ever speak?

The scene continued back and forth for several long minutes. Tighe would send fire and Luke would lift him in the air, slamming him into the invisible wall. Ally was sure they had other abilities, but they seemed to be bent on annoying each other with these specific ones. Both of them glistened with sweat, and she could see their arms shaking from exhaustion.

If she hadn't been so intent on watching Tighe's glowing hands on their fifth go around, she might not have noticed it. Just before his hands reached their full power, he flicked his arm back toward them. It was slight, and barely there, but she saw it.

A signal.

Before she had time to react the male to her left grabbed a hold of her wrist and turned it quickly to the right. Not enough to break the bone, but enough to send a shooting pain up her arm. She was unable to smother the cry that came out of her throat. Tears filled her eyes as she clutched her wrist, which the Exceptional had now released. He stared forward as if nothing had happened.

It had been enough though. Luke faltered, his eyes snapping in her direction, and at that moment Tighe thrust the fireball in his direction. Luke made an attempt to move, but he wasn't fast enough. The fireball consumed the entire right side of his body and he cried out in pain, his body crumpling to the ground. Ally screamed and jumped up. She tried to run to him but her Exceptional bodyguards took a hold of her arms. Tears rolled down her cheeks as they pulled her back to the bench, and a strange sensation tingled in her fingers.

"Luke!" she screamed out, watching as Pax and Maver entered the Arena. The Ref called the match, naming Tighe the winner. Pax pulled a bottle from a bag by his side and began to rub an ointment on Luke's burns. Already he was looking better. Ally had forgotten how quickly Exceptionals healed.

It was five agonizing minutes before Luke was able to stand and meet Tighe in the middle of the Arena. They shook hands and Ally could tell by the expression on Luke's face that this was not over. He glanced over Tighe's shoulder at her, a sorry look filling his face. He had not expected to lose, not at all.

She was forced to stand and step into the area. Tighe's hand slipped around her waist and she watched as Luke's eyes filled with anger and then jealousy. She wondered what plans Tighe had for her, and felt bile rise in her throat at the notion. The Ref spoke out about how Ally was now under contract with Tighe since Luke had lost the fight. The deal was definitive unless they chose to have a rematch on a future date. She kept her eyes on Luke's, and he held her gaze as well.

"I'll find you," he spoke, not seeming to care if Tighe heard him.

Tighe started to pull her from the ring but she resisted, still trying to face Luke. "Please. Don't let him do this."

"I… can't…" Luke's face look pained. She wondered if he were fighting to control the urge to run after her, because all she wanted to do right now was break free and run into his arms.

Ally continued to pull against Tighe's grasp, her whole body vibrating with adrenaline. A hot feeling coursed through her veins and her head was buzzing with pressure. She had never felt this way before, but bit-by-bit she found that rather than being pulled, she was doing the pulling. Tighe turned to look at her, a confused look filling his face.

"Enough," he growled. He threw his arms around her and started to lift her off the ground.

The buzzing energy in her started to gather in her chest and her arms felt as if they were going to burst into flames. She gave one last push against Tighe and as she did, a blinding white light shot from the palms of her hands. Tighe was thrown backwards, flying through the air and landing against the side wall of the Warehouse with a sickening crunch. The crowd around them grew quiet as hushed gasps and whispers spread up the stands. Soon the whole Warehouse was practically silent, as the news carried down to the other end.

Ally looked down at her hands and then back up at Tighe, who had pulled himself off the floor and was strutting toward her. Luke appeared at her side and placed a hand on her shoulder.

"He attacked me!" Tighe looked at the Ref and pointed at Luke, "Outside of the ring. He should be banned from this place."

The Ref stared at Ally with her mouth hanging open, and then looked back at Tighe. "I was standing right here. Luke didn't attack you, it was the girl."

Ally glanced at her hands once again and then this time looked back up at Luke.

"What does this mean?"

Luke's eyes met her own. "It means you're an Exceptional."

Chapter Seventeen

Luke acted fast, taking Ally's hand and rushing her from the Warehouse. The majority of the crowed was still watching them with interest, and he knew he needed to get her out of there before Tighe could fully react to her attack. Pax and Maver caught up to them quickly.

"What's going on?" Pax asked. "What happened back there?"

"I don't know!" Luke said with a bite in his tone.

"This doesn't make sense," Maver added. "I've never seen anything like that before."

Luke ran his hands through his hair. "I need to get her home before others follow us out here, especially Tighe."

He convinced Pax and Maver to head to their own homes, telling them that he would contact them when he could. He didn't want to pull them into this mess, if it would even turn into one. He didn't speak to Ally as they hurried through the streets. He had to assume she was in some sort of shock, and he needed to get her home before she either broke down or used her abilities again.

Once they were safely inside his house, he locked the front door behind them and dropped Ally's hand, leaning up against the wall. His father had been practically living at the office these days, and his mother was most likely holed up in her bedroom. The last thing he needed was for either of them to take in the sight of Ally and start questioning what had happened.

"Luke—" Ally's voice sounded strained.

"Ally!" Sabine came running into the room, fresh tears running

166

down her cheeks. "Asher! Ally is here!"

Asher ran into the room, skidding to a stop in the foyer. Relief fell on his face, and when he caught a glimpse of Luke, he lowered his face to the ground.

"Oh Ally." Sabine approached her, throwing her arms around Ally's neck. "I'm so sorry. I wish there had been something we could have done. We sent Flint out to find Luke as soon as we got back, but it looks like you found him first."

Luke watched as Ally took a deep breath and managed to compose herself. "Well, I'm okay now. Tighe took me to the Warehouse, and right to Luke. As you can see, I'm in one piece."

He was glad that she was at least able to speak and respond to the others.

Sabine pulled away from her and smiled. "I knew one way or another Luke would bring you home. I'll go tell Mazzi to get dinner started."

Luke took a hold of Ally's hand and pulled her towards the stairs. "Tell Mazzi to send some food up the chute to my room."

He had competed in— and won— three fights before Tighe had shown up at the Warehouse. He was feeling more run down than usual, and on top of it his side was still healing from the burns Tighe had inflicted on him. He had never lost focus like that in a fight before.

Once he was satisfied that his bedroom door was locked behind them, he turned to find Ally running her hands along the white comforter on his bed. She was looking much healthier these days, already gaining weight back from her time at the ORC. She wore her hair braided to the side today and it hung over the front of her gray shirt.

"We are going to need to get you a set of white uniforms now,"

167

he joked.

Ally turned to him, a concerned look on her face. "We should talk about this."

He nodded. "Yes, but there is something I need to do first."

She clasped her hands together in front of her. "What's that?"

With out another word he walked toward her, slowly at first and then with more purpose. He gently placed a hand on either side of her face and leaned toward her slowly.

"Luke—," she whispered.

"I could have lost you today," he said as he pressed his mouth to hers. The thought had run through his mind a dozen times since Tighe presented her in the Warehouse.

Ally broke from the kiss first, looking up at him. "I'm so sorry that I didn't listen to you this morning. I should have trusted you and taken your words seriously. I risked everything we have just to run errands with Sabine and Asher."

He wrapped his arms around her and pulled her into a hug. "I should have explained the *why* more. I shouldn't expect you to heed to everything I ask of you. Let's just be thankful it turned out how it did."

"Can we really though?" She looked down at her hands. "What is happening to me?"

Luke took a hand and cupped her chin, forcing her to look at him. Her large green eyes shown brightly, and as he took a closer look, he noticed sparkling, violet flecks.

"Somehow, you are becoming an Exceptional. I don't know how, but you are." He stepped back and took a seat on his bed.

Ally sat down as well. "What I did back at the Warehouse… is that normal?"

"I'm not sure Ally. Our abilities develop when we are young and slowly grow as we progress. What you did to Tighe... that is a strong ability, especially for someone your age. But it could just be that all of the energy has been harnessed somewhere deep within you and was finally unleashed. It isn't completely abnormal for an Exceptional's first display of power to be a big one."

She nodded her head. "But how? I've always been an Ordinary. My mom is an Ordinary; my dad was an Ordinary, and Stosh... oh. Stosh is my twin, Luke. Do you think he is experiencing these changes too?"

"If he does, the Guards will find him and bring him in. He won't be able to hide his abilities for long. He'll need to learn to control them, especially if he is spilling over with power like you were."

He didn't mention that he had seen Stosh just a day prior, and Stosh had looked Ordinary enough, displaying no signs of Exceptional abilities. He had been angry enough with Luke that if he had abilities, he would have used them then.

"What happens now?" she asked, leaning her head against his shoulder.

"You'll need to be trained at the Institute. It won't be long until word of what happened in the Warehouse gets back to my father, and he'll make sure you attend."

Ally cringed. "I really don't want to deal with Aden again."

"You won't have a choice, but at least now you'll have more rights. You can get your own home and all. You'll never have to go back to the ORC, or be controlled. If Tighe had left with you this evening—" He stopped talking, unable to finish his thought.

"What if I want to stay here with you?"

"I'd be okay with that," he smiled. "Can you control it, do you know? Could you use your ability again if I asked you to, right now?"

Ally flexed her hands into fists and then straightened her fingers out again. "I don't think so. Just before I, whatever it is that I did, I felt a vibrating sensation inside. I actually felt the energy move through my body, down my arms, and out through my fingers. I don't feel any of that now."

Luke knew exactly what she was talking about. It was the same feeling he— and all other Exceptionals— felt right before he used his abilities. For some, it was described as a soft tingling, where others said it felt like their insides were on fire.

Ally continued, "I think it was because I was so angry. I was mad at myself for putting myself in that situation, and mad at Tighe for trying to drag me out of the Warehouse. I felt the buzzing sensation before the fight even began, and I think the adrenaline emanating from the other Exceptionals in the Warehouse helped fuel the energy inside me."

Luke was worried about Ally. Worried about what this meant for her to become an Exceptional this late in her life. Had the virus come back and infected her? If so, all the Ordinarys in the City would be Exceptionals soon, as well as in the settlements. That would be a large amount of uncontrolled abilities. Otherwise, she could be an isolated case, which made less sense. On top of it all, her ability had shown itself as a strong one. And where there was an Exceptional with a strong ability, his father was also.

Ally placed her hand on his arm. "Luke, I know this is a random thing to ask, but have you found anything out about Willow?"

Luke wasn't sure what had caused this to slip into her mind but he was pleased that he could at least give her an answer she would be glad to hear.

"Yes. I found out while I was at the Warehouse today, before you arrived. She isn't far from here, actually. She is assigned to a male Exceptional just a year older than me. His name is Coarse."

"Coarse," she let his name roll slowly off her tongue. "We need to go get her."

"Let me talk to him at the Institute tomorrow. He is training in the medical program there. I might have a better chance of talking him into handing her over to me, rather than if we just showed up on his doorstep tonight."

"Do you think he'll listen?" Ally lowered herself onto the bed.

"It is worth a try."

Luke stood and went to his dresser, getting clean clothes out. As much as he wanted to collapse into bed and sleep, he needed a hot shower more. Ally seemed perfectly content to stare at the ceiling, absentmindedly twirling a strand of her hair. He went into his bathroom and turned on the shower, setting the temperature almost as hot as it would go. The heat didn't bother his Exceptional skin.

As he pulled his shirt over his head he could feel the soreness in his muscles. The left side of his body, the side that had been hit by the flames, was still pink but the skin felt fine when he touched it. He undressed completely and climbed into the shower, letting the hot water engulf him. The injured area of his body tingled under the heat, but not enough to make him turn the temperature down. He made his shower quick, drying off and putting on a fresh pair of pajamas.

He leaned on the counter, staring at his reflection in the mirror. His hair had grown out enough that the ends hung over his hairline, small beads of water forming on the ends. Tomorrow he would have to explain the events of today to his friends, and most likely his father. He had always revolted against the system, forcing himself to be unaffected by all the conditions his father put into place. He didn't want to be a City leader, mainly; he didn't want to be anything like his father. But now, doing just that might be the very thing that could keep Ally safe.

Not only could he make her happy by shutting down the ORC and changing the way the Exceptionals viewed Ordinarys, but he could also ensure that no one ever brought harm to her again. He didn't know if the Exceptional part of her they saw today would stay, and if it didn't, he was going to be prepared to fight for her.

By the time he stepped back into his bedroom, he found Ally curled up on her side, fast asleep. She looked vulnerable lying there, her facial features softer than usual. The corner of her mouth curved down slightly, reminding Luke of the emotional pain she had been holding inside since he brought her here. She might seem happy on the outside, but deep down she missed her family and the life she once had. He thought about settling down on the couch but decided the only place he wanted to be right now was close to Ally. He carefully repositioned her so that she was under the covers, and slid in quietly beside her. He wrapped his arm around her, pulling her close. He knew one thing for sure; he never wanted to let her go again.

Chapter Eighteen

Ally was back in the settlement, returning home after a long day of gathering. She had met her food quota by almost twice the amount, and felt at the top of her game. Tomorrow she would have a free day, and perhaps she and Stosh could go for a run like old times.

When she stepped through the front door of her house, she could already smell her mother's cooking. She was making a rabbit stew tonight, probably accompanied by fresh made bread from their monthly wheat ration. Stosh was out back cleaning up after a long day of wood chopping, and the family they lived with was already gathered in the dining room, setting the table for dinner.

Ally stepped into the kitchen and helped her mother prepare the last of the meal, carrying a pot of stew to the table. But when they sat down to eat, it wasn't stew that she had been carrying, but a large platter of cooked ham. Stosh hopped into the house and took a seat, dishing himself up a big portion of glazed carrots. There were even mashed potatoes on the table, with a big slab of butter on top. It wasn't a meal that Ally had ever eaten in the settlement before, but somehow she knew she had tried these foods before tonight.

No one spoke. Rather, everyone at the table smiled at each other numbly and stuffed their faces. Ally found that she couldn't speak, even though she really wanted to. After they had eaten all the food, she and Stosh did the dishes and cleaned up the dining room. Stosh wandered off to his own room, and the family they lived with had disappeared. Ally carried a small bucket of water in from the well out back, wanting to clean up before she headed to bed as well. She pulled her hair back from her face and splashed cool water over her skin, letting it wash away the dirt and grime. She dried her face on a towel and slowly looked up into a mirror.

She jumped at what she saw. A female Exceptional was staring back her, her violet eyes shimmering in the dim light. Ally raised her hand toward the mirror, and the Exceptional did the same. Ally touched her face and watched as the Exceptional copied her movements. Ally was annoyed at first, but as she looked at the female Exceptional closer, she came to a frightening realization.

The Exceptional in the mirror was her.

Ally's eyes popped open and she found that she was breathing heavily. That was the first time she had dreamt so vividly of home, and she hoped it would be the last.

THE BLINDS had been open the previous night and as a result, sunlight bathed across the bed and warmed Ally's skin. She turned her head slightly, catching a glimpse of Luke lying next to her. He was on his stomach, with one arm thrown over her waist and the other up under his pillow. His head was facing the opposite direction but his deep breathing told her that he was still asleep. She settled her head back on the soft pillow and looked up at the white ceiling.

The events of yesterday rushed back into her mind. She was still having trouble sorting through her feelings and deciding exactly how to process this. How much *bad* news could a person handle in such a short period of time? She had handled coming into the City with some dignity since she had grown up knowing that she might one day volunteer to go. The ORC had thrown her for a loop, but despite her emotional time there, she was able to come back to Luke and find a way to move on. But becoming an Exceptional? This was something she never could have prepared for, because it had never been heard of. Also, being in Luke's bed *with* Luke was doing funny things to her insides.

She tried to shake the image of kissing Luke from her mind.

Today she needed to focus on her new abilities, and what they meant for her future. She planned on asking Luke to take her to the Institute with him this morning. He had said that Aden would force her to go in for testing and training anyway, so she might as well start now.

Luke stirred beside her, turning his head and opening his eyes. He smiled at her and the sight sent warmth running through her body.

"Good morning," he said in a scratchy voice.

Ally couldn't help but grin. "Morning."

Luke leaned forward and pressed his mouth to hers, softly kissing her. Rather than pulling away, like he normally did, he intensified the kiss, pressing into her. She wound her arms up around his back and dug her fingers into his hair, pulling him closer. He was propped up on his elbows now, hovering over her, but she could tell he didn't plan to get any closer. This felt dangerous enough, and it wasn't helping her keep focus like she had planned to do just moments ago.

A knock on the door forced them to jump apart. Ally smoothed her hair down while Luke stood and walked over to the door, unlocking it. She watched him stiffen as he opened the door, and when he stepped backward his expression held none of the joy it did just a minute earlier.

"Father," he said as moved aside so that Aden could enter.

Aden peered around the room and gave a small chuckle when he found Ally in Luke's bed. "I hear you've been busy, Allona."

Sure, now that she was an Exceptional she was worthy of a real name.

"I'm not sure what you are talking about," she said with a shrug, acting as though nothing worth talking about had happened to her lately.

"It's very curious that you were able to delay your Exceptional powers all these years. Also curious is how you were able to look and act like an Ordinary as well."

"You think I did this on purpose?" Her tone was sour.

Aden's expression didn't change. "I didn't say any such thing, but the mere fact that you are mentioning it doesn't look very good, Allona."

"Stop calling me that!" she yelled at him. She rarely lost control, but he managed to bring out the worst in her with a mere minute of conversation.

"I am not here to accuse you of anything, *Ally*, but I am going to need you to come with me. You'll be taken to the Institute immediately, where we'll be running some tests."

"I can take her there today when I go for lessons." Luke stepped forward.

"Not necessary." Aden waved his hand. "I'm headed there right now and would be pleased to escort her."

Ally hopped out of bed, thinking that the faster she showed she was willing to work with him, the faster he would go away. "I'll shower, get dressed, and meet you in the foyer in twenty minutes."

"I like this new air of cooperation from you, Ally." Aden smirked and left the room.

"He's up to something." Luke's brows were furrowed together as he spoke.

"Like you've said before, there isn't much we can do. I'm going to get ready and go with him. At least maybe we'll get some answers." She stretched her arms above her head and made a move for Luke's bathroom.

"Oh, I guess I can go back to my own room now." She laughed, stepping toward the door. Each morning she would rise and leave the room before Luke woke, changing in her own room. Using his bathroom and changing in his space felt more intimate than they were already being, which wasn't very intimate at all compared to what the ORC contract said they *should* be doing.

Luke caught her around the waist and pulled her in for another kiss. "Nonsense. Go start your shower and I'll have Sabine bring fresh clothes to you. You've spent the past week sleeping in my room, even if I slept on the sofa, and I consider this space as much yours as it is mine. Although, I'd like it if we shared the space more like we did last night."

Ally felt her cheeks reddened at his words. Luke held back a laugh. "It doesn't have to mean anything more than two people sleeping next to each other in the same bed, Ally."

She sighed and took his hand in hers. "I know."

Something tugged at Ally's insides, making her feel anxious about possible danger in the near future. Did the danger lie in falling in love with Luke, or going to the Institute for training? She looked over at Luke and saw the possibilities shining in his violet eyes. She was an Exceptional, and no matter how scary it seemed, she was a true part of the City now. She could be his with out a contract, and with out scrutiny. It also meant that she was that much further from her family in the settlement. She no longer belonged there and now, she could definitely never return.

EXACTLY NINETEEN MINUTES later Ally was dressed and standing in the foyer. Exactly one minute after that Aden appeared from the kitchen, dressed in a freshly pressed, white suit. As he walked toward her she found it hard not to notice the similarities between Luke and his father. Aden's hair was much longer, since adult Exceptionals weren't required to shave their heads, but she could see the dark shade it used to be hidden underneath a soft blanket of gray. She could even picture Luke wearing a suit just like the one Aden was wearing. She stopped her thoughts before they traveled further, for trying to compare Luke to his father felt wrong.

"There is a transport waiting at the end of the street," Aden said as he motioned for her to follow him out of the house.

Ally had heard of transports before. They were not used often, except for Guards traveling a far distance or in case Aden needed to be taken out of the City quickly. She had even been able to catch a glimpse of one or two in the air in her lifetime. Both times she had been up in a tree back in the settlement, and had been perplexed as the giant object passed overhead. Transports were odd shaped machines with long spindles on top that spun very fast. Somehow those spindles were able to carry the machine through the air, with the help of another set of spindles on the tail. Ally had thought it made an odd sound in the sky, but as they approached the end of the street, she was shocked by how loud it sounded on the ground. Even more shocking was the wind it made and how hard it smacked her in the face.

The transport sat in the middle of a circular part of the street, and several Exceptionals stood outside their homes, watching. From their expressions, Ally could tell this was nothing special to them, but it must be more interesting than whatever else they had planned for their day. Aden took a hold of her arm and led her through the strong wind, helping her up into the main area of the transport. Once inside Aden handed her an odd shaped piece of equipment. She watched as he placed an identical object on his head and over his ears, and she did the same. She almost sighed the relief was so great. She could barely hear the sound of the transport with these things covering her ears.

"They are called headphones." He pointed at the object on his head. "We'll be taking off now, it will be a little bumpy to start."

Aden's voice filled her ears and her hands flew up to the object he had called headphones. She watched as he spoke into a small object near his mouth, and realized it was sending the words through the headphones. A similar object sat near her mouth so she decided to test it out.

"I've never seen transports at the Institute before. Couldn't we have walked?" As interesting as this was becoming, she didn't like the idea of trusting a machine to carry her through the air.

"We won't be going to the Institute." He sat back in his seat and peered out the window as the transport lifted off the ground.

Ally grabbed a hold of a handle near her head and looked out the opposite window. Luke had been right; Aden was definitely up to something.

THE RIDE didn't take long, and Ally spent most of it staring at the people and buildings below. The tallest building in the City Center, which stood at twelve stories tall, loomed up in front of them and the transport lifted above it. She took hold of the handle again as it lowered onto the roof with a bump. Aden popped the door open and motioned for her to leave the headphones behind. The Exceptional who had been flying the transport did something to power the machine down, and the loud chopping sound slowly disappeared.

Aden didn't wait for Ally to exit the transport before he started toward a door positioned at one end of the roof. Two Exceptional Guards took a place on either side of her and escorted her behind him, their guns held firmly at their chests. She was led into a dimly lit staircase and down two flights of stairs. They entered through a black door with no markings, stepped across a dark hallway, and walked into a large open room.

Ally found herself surprised by the stark difference between this room and the ones back at Aden's home. Almost everything in this room was a dark color, except for the walls, which were painted white. A black rug filled the floor, along with black tables, sofas, and a desk. She realized that she must be in Aden's office, and it took up at least half of the entire floor. To her right was a wall of windows, which Aden's desk sat right in front of. To her left was a wall with several doors, which must lead to meeting rooms.

Aden motioned to the guards. "Go get Dr. Leon and Dr. Axel for me. I want them to meet their newest test subject."

"So why come here rather than the Institute?" Ally stepped over to one of the black couches and sat on the back of it, facing Aden.

He walked over to his desk and pressed a button on the side. A cup appeared from a chute in the wall, steam coming off the contents in it. It was most likely hot tea, a drink favored by many adults. Since it was expensive, their mom only drank it once or twice a year. Aden could probably afford to drink it several times a day.

"I think it will be more favorable for us to run the tests here. The Institute is busy and filled with teenage Exceptionals all day long, and it lacks the type of security I believe we will require today. I'm also not naïve enough to think that Luke wouldn't have tried to find us as soon as he arrived. Here, I have much more control."

Ally raised one eyebrow. "You don't think that Luke will figure out what you've done? He probably heard, if not saw, the transport."

Aden shrugged. "Yes, but it will be much harder for him to gain access to my office. I have no doubts that he will show up here sooner rather than later, and at the right time I will allow him to come up."

She decided to change the subject. "These tests you'll be running. Are they anything like the tests I had at the ORC?"

Aden's lips paused on his mug and his violet eyes slowly rose to meet hers. "You know, they mentioned that they thought you might be avoiding your medication while at the ORC. And I'm guessing they didn't do a memory swipe before you left?"

Ally hadn't realized there would be a memory swipe, but she was sure Luke had something to do with putting a stop to it. "It might have been overlooked. What I want to know is *why* you are breeding Ordinarys with Exceptionals."

Aden laughed loudly, setting his cup down on his desk. He strode toward Ally and stopped just a foot in front of her. "This is much bigger than you or any of your little Ordinary friends, so I suggest that you drop it."

His expression grew so fierce that Ally found herself leaning away from him, any possible response she had caught in her throat. Just when she thought she had recomposed herself enough to speak, the two Exceptional Guards from earlier reentered the room. Behind them came two male Exceptionals, both dressed in long white coats similar to the medical professionals in the ORC.

"Dr. Leon. Dr. Axel." Aden greeted them.

One of the doctors approached Ally immediately. "Hello Allona. I'm Dr. Leon. I am the head of the EGD at the Institute."

"EGD?" she asked.

"Exceptional Genetics Department. I study our DNA, looking for changing patterns or further mutations." His silver eyes studied hers intently, making her uncomfortable.

The second Exceptional stepped forward. "And I'm Dr. Axel, head of the Research Department. I've spent years looking for a way to recreate the serum that blessed us with Exceptionals, and also ways to keep possible vaccinations at bay. And here, you've been right outside our grasp all this time."

Ally laughed. "You think I'm the key to your serum?"

Dr. Axel's expression never changed. "I hope so."

"I'm guessing that I have no choice but to become a test subject for your doctors here," Ally said as she turned to Aden.

Aden smiled. "There is always a choice, Ally. But I think I can persuade you into helping us."

"So there *isn't* a choice." She crossed her arms over her chest. "What will you use to persuade me?"

Aden nodded at the Exceptional Guards and they disappeared into the hall. The doctors stepped aside and Aden went back to his desk, so it appeared as though she was going to have to wait for whatever the persuasion was. Just a few minutes later a shuffling sound came from the hall. A woman yelped and Ally heard a male voice curse, most likely at one of the Guards.

She froze. Her heart beat so loud and fast that it sounded loud enough to be right between her ears rather that in her chest. She counted the agonizing seconds it took the Guards to reach the doors and watched in horror as they pushed her mother and Stosh into the room.

182

"So, Ally," Aden said from a reclined position in his chair, "Are you going to *choose* to help us?"

Chapter Nineteen

It took Ally's mother and Stosh a moment to realize where they were, and who they were looking at.

"Ally?" her mother whispered.

Ally ran forward and embraced her family all at once, tears slipping down her cheeks and soaking Stosh's shirt. She pulled back and smiled, feeling as though a weight had been lifted from her shoulders. She thought she would never see them again, and here they were, standing right in front of her. She noticed that Stosh wouldn't look at her, his expression hard and his gaze fixated on the wall behind them. Her mother took her hand, squeezing it tightly within her own.

There was so much she wanted to say to them, but she didn't have time to form the words. Aden cleared his throat from his desk, a smug expression on his face.

"What are they doing here?" Ally turned to face him.

When I heard about the incident at the Warehouse last night, I thought that maybe bringing your family in would help you be more compliant."

"What do you want?" she said through gritted teeth.

"First, I want some answers. Then, I want you to comply with the tests my team of doctors are going to put you through over the next couple days. They may not all be very... pleasant."

"Of course not," Ally shook her head. "I'll do it. You just have to promise not to harm them, and to send them back to the settlement when this is all over."

"Sure," Aden responded, but something flickered in his eyes. He didn't like being told what to do. Ally knew that things had to be done on his terms, but she had to take a chance. She hadn't missed the fact that he hadn't exactly promised her anything.

He stood, grabbed a fresh cup of hot tea, and led them to the other end of the room. They were ushered through a doorway and into a small meeting room, which was set up with a table in the middle with a dozen chairs surrounding it. Ally, Stosh, and their mother sat on one side of the table, while Aden and the doctors sat on the other.

"We'll start with you, Stosh," Aden leaned forward, his eyes narrowing as he scrutinized Ally's brother. "Dr. Leon?" he added.

The doctor stood and walked around the table, sitting in one of the empty chairs next to Stosh. Ally could read her brother, and knew that he was moments away from losing it. His hands were clenched into fists by his side, and small veins stood up along his neck. She placed her hand on his arm, hoping the gesture would help him relax.

Ally was worried about him. He looked thinner than he had before she had left, and sometime recently he had used sheers to give himself a very bad buzz cut. It was so short that he could almost fit in with the other Exceptionals boys here. Of course, she had changed as well. She was thinner, from her time at the ORC, and there was the big change she hadn't announced yet. She was an Exceptional. Maybe that was why he could barely look at her right now, or why her mother was still sobbing to herself: Aden had told them about her abilities.

"He doesn't appear to be one of us," Dr. Leon finally said, looking very disappointed. Aden and Dr. Axel wore similar expressions on their face. "A blood test will tell us for sure".

"What do you mean one of *you*?" Stosh growled. "We're all

human."

Ally squeezed Stosh's arm, giving him a silent warning.

"What Dr. Leon meant to say is that you are not an Exceptional, like your sister here," Aden spoke in an annoyingly calm voice.

"So it's true," Stosh finally faced Ally, looking at her directly for the first time since they were reunited. "You're an Exceptional?"

Ally swallowed back tears, nodding her head. "At least, we think so."

Aden ignored their private conversation and moved on. "And you, Luella," he addressed Ally's mother. "You are obviously not an Exceptional, which means either Ally is not your daughter, or you've been telling her lies about her father."

A chill ran up Ally's spine. She hadn't had time to think about what this meant for her family, or what the truth behind her abilities might be. She had momentarily worried about Stosh's fate, but that had been it. He was her brother; she knew it. Forget the fact that they looked and acted exactly alike, but she could feel it deep within. They had a bond only twins could share.

Their mother grew quiet, her gaze stuck on Aden's. Ally could see how he might have a powerful effect on someone who hadn't been around Exceptionals much in the past several years. But her mother sat up straighter and rubbed the tears from underneath her eyes.

"He was one of your Guards, passing through the settlement to gather volunteers. There was a blizzard that year, and whiteout conditions stalled the caravan from moving through." Ally tightened her grip on her Stosh's arm. "We were asked to take in Guards if we had the room, and I did at the time. I think you can figure the rest out, Aden."

Ally wanted to cheer on her mom for using his first name so

loosely, and with a tone of contempt, but she remained silent. The story her mother told made butterflies take flight in her stomach. What details was her mother leaving out? What exactly happened that night with the Exceptional Guard?

"Interesting," was all Aden could respond with. "You fell pregnant with twins, and one turned out to be an Ordinary, and the other an Exceptional."

The doctors had both pulled out porta-comps and were typing in information at a dizzying pace. Ally noticed that Stosh was watching them with growing interest.

"That still doesn't explain why Ally hasn't exhibited any abilities until now."

Ally's mother kept her gaze on Aden, shrugging her shoulders. "Isn't that what your tests will find out?"

Aden gave a humorless grin, his hand dipping into his pocket. He pulled out a small handgun, something Ally had only seen a few times in her life. The settlement leaders were each given one in case of an emergency. She had only seen Po use it once, and that was when a wild bear entered the settlement and couldn't be coaxed out. He ended up shooting the bear three times, killing it.

Aden smirked. "You see, I have a theory. One that is going to disappoint my colleagues here, but would be a simple explanation for all of this." Dr. Leon and Dr. Axel looked just as confused as Ally felt. "I think that you used something to suppress the genetic mutations that are currently turning Ally into an Exceptional."

Ally's mother leaned back in her chair, her face turning as white as the walls. "I don't know what you're talking about."

Aden frowned. "I think you do. Long ago, when SS-16 was first created, a scientist was able to discover a vaccine that would cure the infected of the side effects. But what was there to cure? Look at us. We are faster, stronger, and thriving with out wars and famine. The vaccine was destroyed, but there are rumors that the formula was hidden and eventually Ordinarys figured out how to reproduce it. Do you know anything about that?"

"I only know what you just recited to me. My father used to tell me that same story when I was younger."

Aden turned the gun over in his hands, inspecting it for a moment. "I have many abilities, Luella, and one of them happens to be reading people."

He raised the gun and pointed it at their mother's head. Stosh jumped from his chair and leaned across the table, almost managing to grab hold of Aden's throat before one of the doctors used a porta-comp to slam him on the back of the head. Stosh fell limp on the table. Ally attempted to jump in front of her mother but a Guard swept into the room and took hold of her, locking her into his arms. She willed her Exceptional powers to make an appearance, like they did in a similar situation the night before, but she felt no vibrating energy. No heat running through her veins.

"She doesn't know anything, Aden. What are you doing? You promised you would keep them safe," Ally managed to yell out before the Guard placed a hand over her mouth.

Aden laughed. "I don't make promises, Ally, and I definitely don't take orders. We are going to do this my way. Now, Luella…"

Ally's mother sat there in silence, playing with the hem of her black shirt. Her light hair fell in curled ribbons around her face, and her lashes glistened with the remainder of the tears from earlier.

"I know nothing," she whispered.

Ally wasn't sure what brought the memory to her mind at that moment, but she figured it had something to do with the sight of Aden putting his finger over the trigger of the gun. He wouldn't kill her mother, would he? The gun was just a display. A show to scare them. If he really wanted to harm her, he would most likely use his abilities. The answer became clear in an instant, and considering she had even talked to Luke about this, she was surprised neither one of them had thought of it last night.

Ally screamed into the hand of the Guard, trying to get Aden's attention.

Aden nodded and the Guard lifted his hand.

"Shots," she gasped out. "Every six months we received a shot."

She and Stosh had been due to receive a shot around the time she was taken into the City.

Ally's mother shot her a fearful look, her eyes wide. "Ally—"

"Quiet," Aden snapped.

"There is this man, David," Ally spoke quickly. "He lives in the Wilderness, and we would visit him twice a year. He would give both my brother and I a shot. Our mother told us it was to keep away sickness and help us grow up healthy, but we were also told to keep it a secret."

Most of the story was the truth, except for the name and location of the man. David had been her grandfather's name, and he died over ten years ago. But Aden seemed so focused on the information that she hoped he didn't feel any doubt at her words. The last thing she needed was for Aden to tear through her settlement on a wild rampage, looking for this man.

"Where in the Wilderness?" Aden's eyes were glowing.

"Five miles west of our settlement. There is a large pond with a wooden shack at the end. He lives there." There was a pond, and there also happened to be a wooden shack, but no one had lived there in years. It was used as a resting place on summer days spent swimming in the cool water, so there would at least be some signs of life to throw Aden's Guards off for a bit.

"See how easy that was," Aden responded.

Ally took a deep breath, relieved that she had remembered the shots, and saved her mother's life. But just as the relief entered her body, Aden raised the gun higher and pulled the trigger, putting a bullet right between her mother's eyes.

WHEN ALLY AND STOSH turned ten, their mother let them travel into the woods on their own for the first time. They had each been out several times with groups of Ordinarys, training for their assigned tasks, but never just the two of them. The first thing Ally did was climb one of the tallest trees, giggling as she returned to the ground covered in sap and pine needles. Stosh chose to stay on the ground and hunt for pinecones instead.

"Climb a tree with me, Stosh," Ally picked up a small pinecone and threw it at him, hitting him square in the back.

"What if I fall?" He gazed upward, taking in the height of the tree.

"You won't fall, I'll be right there with you!" she giggled.

But he did fall. He fell fifteen feet from the tree, landing in a bed of pine needles below. By the time Ally got to the bottom of the tree, Stosh was jumping around and grasping his wrist. Tears were streaming down his cheeks and he was screaming.

"I told you! I told you!" he shouted as he took off running toward the settlement.

That night, after the doctor set Stosh's broken wrist, their mother sat and rocked Stosh to sleep. She whispered softly in his ear and ran her fingers through his hair. After she had put him to bed and came back to sit by the fire, Ally crouched by her side.

"Does this mean we won't be allowed in the woods anymore, Mother?" She looked at her feet.

Her mother laughed. "Of course you'll be allowed back in the woods, Allona. Accidents happen, and with time you'll learn to prevent them."

"So, I'm not in trouble," she asked, looking up.

Her mother smiled. "Not at all. Just… be more careful with your brother. He is more fragile than you know. You are my strong and courageous one, Allona. One day you'll move mountains."

The memory faded into darkness.

ALLY HAD TO BE SEDATED in order for them to get her under control. After Aden had shot her mother in head, she felt a familiar vibrating feeling in her arms. She ripped herself from the Guards hold and raised her hands toward Aden, pushing all the energy she had out of herself and toward him. He blocked the attack easily, something she should have seen coming, and Dr. Axel was by her side a moment later. He stuck a needle in her arm, and the rest of the details were fuzzy.

Now she was lying on a cold, metal table in a large room with an echo. She knew it echoed because she screamed until her throat was raw and her voice was little more than a rasp. Beside her, Stosh laid on a similar table. He still hadn't woken up from the blow to his head, but Ally could see the rise and fall of his chest as he took breath after breath. At least she didn't lose her whole family today.

Her head still felt heavy from the drugs they had given her, and she had lost all track of time. The room was brightly lit but had no windows that she could see from the position she was in. No one had even been in to see her or her brother. Maybe, now that Aden had his answer, he would send Guards into the Wilderness to look for "David". They wouldn't find him there, and when Aden realized that, he would come back to her looking for more information.

There was also the fact that she had abilities, and strong ones. Aden had been able to see them firsthand when she tried to use them against him, and now he most likely had big plans for her future. She also knew exactly why her brother was still alive, stationed just out of her grasp. Aden planned to use him against her, just like he used her against Luke in the Institute. One way or another, he always got exactly what he wanted.

A door opened behind her head, and she laid still. Had they come to take Stosh? Had they come to take her? Ally had no fight left; her body felt depleted and her mind numb from the death of her mother.

"I think the sedation has worn off enough," a female Exceptional said, leaning over her.

Ally heard something metal clang to her right. "I've been instructed to draw some blood and take a tissue sample, and they wanted you fully aware for the procedure."

Ally didn't respond. She kept her eyes trained on the bright lights above and waited. The nurse dabbed something cold into the crease in Ally's arm and tied a piece of cloth tightly above the same area. Ally had her blood drawn several times in her time at the ORC, so this felt all too familiar. A quick skin prick later and the nurse was filling four vials with blood.

"This part will hurt a little worse," the woman said.

She lifted a sharp instrument in the air and leaned over Ally's arm. Ally cried out as the blade sliced into her arm, a white-hot pain filling her senses. Since she was making the change into an Exceptional, her nerves wouldn't be as sensitive, so she wondered what this would have felt like if she were still an Ordinary.

The woman kept the blade in place and used another instrument to retrieve the tissue sample she had cut out of Ally's arm. She put the instruments back on the tray, released the cloth tie, and bandaged the wound.

"Aden asked me to sedate you once I was done," the woman used her fingers to flick a syringe in her hand. "I hope you'll understand."

Again, Ally saw no need to speak. It wasn't as though she had any choice in what was happening to her. *You always have a choice*, Aden had told her. Yes, but only if the choice benefited him. She felt a small pinch on her arm and soon a heavy veil of darkness was sweeping over her.

Chapter Twenty

Luke knew the moment Aden left the house with Ally that they wouldn't be going to the Institute. No, Ally would be taken to his father's office in the City Center. He worried about what Aden had planned for her, but if he wanted any hope of getting in to see her, he would need to play by his father's rules. With that in mind, he headed straight to the Institute once he was ready, arriving early for his first lesson. Today he would focus on training sessions, which would mean more exercises to increase his abilities. After the previous night's drain on his energy, he could already tell his trainer was going to be disappointed with his work. He went through the motions in his lessons, getting by with average work and progress.

It was as he was preparing to leave the Institute that he remembered his promise to Ally. He fought the urge to leave the building anyway and go straight to her, but he doubted Aden would be allowing her to go anywhere anytime soon. He slipped into the cafeteria and peered around the room, looking for his target.

"Hey Luke, glad to see you up and walking after last night," an Exceptional he recognized, Drexel, slapped him on the shoulder as he passed by.

He spotted Pax and Maver but pretended not to notice them. He knew they would have a ton of questions about Ally, and would want to trail along with him to his father's building. Finally he spotted Coarse sitting at a table along the back wall of windows. Three other

194

Exceptionals sat with him. Luke strode across the room and stopped at their table.

"Coarse," he said, not acknowledging the others.

Coarse looked up from his food. Even though he was still attending the Institute as a medical student, he was technically considered an adult Exceptional now. He displayed his status by having allowed his hair to grow out. It fell in dark curls around his face.

"Luke," he responded. "I heard about last night."

Luke shook his head. "That isn't what I'm here to talk about. I would prefer if we spoke in private, though."

Coarse nodded to the others, who stood and left. Luke took a seat directly across from him.

"I heard you've recently acquired an Ordinary from ORC." Luke leaned back in his chair and set his hands on the table.

Coarse smirked. "Yeah. What's it to you?"

"This Ordinary has certain interests to me."

Coarse laughed. "This isn't the Warehouse, Luke. I'm not going to barter."

Luke leaned forward. "All I'm asking is that you pass her along to me. We don't need to settle this in the Warehouse."

He flicked his finger and watched as Coarse's tray rose a few inches into the air and then smacked back down on the table. "Like I said, she has certain interests to me."

Coarse pushed his chair back. "Look, I'd like to help you, Luke. I really would. But I sent her back to the ORC three days ago. If you want her, you can go get her yourself."

He stood and grabbed his tray, leaving Luke and the almost empty table behind. Luke groaned and turned around to catch a glimpse

195

of his friends. He was going to need their help after all.

AN HOUR LATER, and much later than he would have liked, Luke stormed into his father's office. He had been surprised how easily the Guards let him pass, but then again, he was sure his father was expecting him.

"Luke." Aden sat at his desk, a porta-comp in his hands. "You arrived much later than I thought you would."

"I had a few things to take care of," Luke responded, stepping further into the room. "Where is she?"

"Sedated." Aden said in a tone that suggested he was bored with the thought.

"Sedated?" Luke's body went stiff. "What did you do to her?"

"I didn't do anything to *her*," he grinned.

"Enough with the word games. Tell me what happened." Luke threw himself into a chair on the other side of his father's desk.

"There was a misunderstanding with her family. That is all." He shrugged.

"Her family? You didn't bring them here, did you?" Luke felt anger bubbling up inside him. Ally's family meant everything to her. He should have known that his father would find a way to use them against her.

"I found it necessary," Aden said, turning his porta-comp off.

"And?" Luke still didn't understand why Ally was under sedation.

Aden motioned behind him. Luke turned his head and for the first time noticed a group of Exceptionals gathered around one of the meeting rooms. Two medics pulled a portable hospital bed from the room. A bloodied sheet hung over what was obviously a human body.

Luke jumped up, energy vibrating through his arms. "Who?"

"Her mother."

Luke felt the energy explode from his palms as he threw his father up against the window behind his desk. The glass barely moved, having been specifically made for ensuring Aden's safety, but Luke still felt some satisfaction at the sound his father's body made as he hit it. He could sense the Guards making a move behind him, so while still using one hand to hold his father in place; he used the other to send the Guards flying backward into the far wall.

"You're getting stronger." Aden's eye glowed with pleasure. He didn't fight back against Luke, or struggle against his hold.

"I could kill you," Luke responded.

"But you won't." Aden spoke the truth. Luke couldn't kill his father, despite what he had done.

"Does all of this have something to do with the ORC?" He released his hold on his father, noticing that his arms felt weaker than usual.

"ORC?" Aden said the name of the place carefully, but there was a hint of worry in his tone. "Why would this have anything to do with ORC? That facility has been functioning normally and with out issue for almost ten years now."

"And I've never thought to question it until recently," Luke responded. "Until Ally."

Aden slammed his hand down on the table. "These questions are what destroy whole societies, Luke. People start to doubt, and soon they feel as though they can't trust their leaders. Then they revolt, and we have a war on our hands. You remember what happened to the City

197

in the south."

The southern City was one rarely talked about, and Luke was surprised to hear his father mention it out loud. Almost all Exceptionals and Ordinarys had cut it out of stories, training their memories to forget it. Four Cities stood after the world crumbled around the SS-16 virus. The virus that made Exceptionals what they were today. The City to the south started out just like the others; with the Exceptionals rebuilding and the Ordinarys being assigned to labor forces. But a group of Ordinarys revolted against the system, claiming they had just as many rights as the Exceptionals. They wanted to live in the City as equals. The leaders laughed in their faces and sent them back to their settlements. Soon the Ordinarys were able to convince several Exceptional Guards to join their side in the revolt, and to help them bring down the leaders.

Exactly one year later, the southern City crumbled to the ground with the war between the two sides. Dozens of Exceptionals and Ordinarys were able to escape and travel to one of the other three cities, but their memories had been wiped upon arrival. The leaders of each City met and decided that they would allow Ordinarys into the cities to work, but they would still be a lesser people. They also made the decision to cut off communication with each other and become their own unified cities. They feared that communication would lead to curiosity and greed, and possibly land wars in the future.

"I'm not trying to raise questions in others, Father." Luke sat back down, making an attempt to regain his strength. He might need it yet today. "*I* want to know. I need you to trust me, and tell me what is going on. You say you want me to lead the City with you some day. If that's true, you need to explain things to me."

198

Aden narrowed his eyes. "I'm not sure you have the City's best interest at heart."

"I'm more concerned with Ally's best interests."

"Exactly," Aden sneered, still standing by the window.

"But maybe these interests are one and the same." Luke probed for information. "I plan on being with Ally forever, and if I'm going to be the City leader one day, she is going to be by my side while I do it."

Aden sighed and brought his hand to his forehead, the lines of his face visibly creasing. It was one of the weaker moments Luke had ever seen from his father.

"I'll need to show you." He pulled his key card from his pocket and waited for Luke to stand. "But I'm warning you now, you are not going to like what you see."

Aden led him down the hall and into the elevator. He inserted his key card into a slot in the wall and they moved downward several floors. Rather than the doors opening from the way they came in, a door in the back of the elevator slid open. Luke had ridden in this elevator dozens of times and had never noticed that it opened on both sides.

They stepped into a bright, white hallway void of windows and pictures. Two doors, one on each end, were all that filled the space. Aden took a left and led Luke down the hall, using his key card to gain access through the door at the end. Two Exceptional Guards stood waiting on the other side, and they required Aden and Luke to do thumb scans and have their internal tags checked. They even had their fingers pricked and droplets of their blood were tested for DNA matches. Luke had never seen his father succumb to these checkpoints before. He was normally allowed access to any part of the City with out question.

"As you can see," Aden looked over his shoulder, almost as though he read Luke's mind. "This requires the highest security precautions we have."

The Guards moved to let them pass and they stepped further into the room. The layout was circular, with several large windows spaced evenly around the back half. Machines and test tables were scattered through the middle of the room, and half-dozen doctors wandered around in white lab coats.

One of the doctors, a younger male, saw Aden and approached him immediately. "Sir."

"Dr. Gould," Aden nodded. "I'm assuming you are bringing me further reports on Subject One?"

The doctor's face grew grim. "It isn't looking good, Sir. The experiment we ran has backfired. His genes are mutating at twice the speed."

He spun on his heels and hurried to the first window on the left. Aden followed, motioning for Luke to come as well. Luke stepped beside his father and peered through the window and what he saw made him catch his breath. A human, or at least what remained of one, sat curled up in the corner of a small white room. If he wasn't looking toward them with large, violet eyes, Luke may not have realized that he was some sort of Exceptional. His thin arms were wrapped around his bony legs, and his pointy chin rested on kneecaps that jutted out. His skin had taken on a putrid green color and was so wrinkled it hung off his body in places. What hair he had left hung in ratty knots around his face.

"What happened to him?" Luke placed his hand on the glass.

"Dr. Gould," Aden said, giving the doctor permission to explain.

"What you see here is a Rogue," the doctor started. "An Exceptional whose genes have mutated beyond control. He has no sense of humanity left and is more or less an animal."

"How did this happen?" Luke had never seen or heard of anything like this.

"That is what we are trying to figure out," Aden responded.

"Did he come from the City?"

Dr. Gould paused. "Not technically. He came from *a* City, just not ours."

"Is it an illness?" Luke knew that illnesses were a thing of the past for Exceptionals, but sometimes Ordinarys in the City would fall ill with fevers or a cough.

"No," Aden said as his expression hardened. "It is our future."

LUKE PROCESSED his father's words for several minutes before he hurried to catch up. Aden and Dr. Gould had moved on to window two, where a female Exceptional, or Rogue, sat on a white hospital bed. She had the same discolored skin and patchy hair, and her eyes were starting to turn a muted gray color.

"Our future?" He watched as the female they were observing leaned forward and bit into her pillow, ripping a large chunk of cloth off the cover.

"It took one hundred years for the Exceptional genes to fully evolve to what we are today. The first generations of Exceptionals were strong, but not as strong as we are now. They had extra abilities, but no more than one, where we can have multiple. It would seem that our genes are beginning to evolve further, mutating into what Dr. Gould addressed as a Rogue."

"All of us?" Luke swallowed at a lump in his throat.

"At first we weren't sure," Aden responded. "But then we got a message from the eastern City. It has been almost fifty years since I last heard from the leader there, and just about as long since a roamer came to our City from theirs."

Aden never took his eyes off the female Rogue as he spoke.

"What did it say, the message?" Luke asked.

"It was a distress signal, sent almost a year ago. It started with how they had been experimenting with a new serum, one that would further enhance our DNA. The second half of the message was asking for aid, stating that they were under attack by their own. The message was cut short, and we never heard from them again, even though we sent responses."

"Their own?" Luke thought. "Is that where these Except— Rogues are from?"

Aden nodded. "We believe that whatever serum they came up with unleashed a new virus. They probably had no idea what was happening until it was too late to contain the infected. We sent a patrol six months ago to survey the situation."

"What did you find?" Luke prompted, trying to keep the conversation moving.

"We found the City in complete disarray. Their City is smaller than ours, but runs very similarly. There were a dozen settlements outside their boundary wall, and we found that they were completely empty of life. There were several signs that the Ordinarys had made a hasty exit, but there was also bloodshed," Aden paused. "The City was overrun with Rogues. We flew a transport overhead and were able to capture images of them tearing into buildings and houses, creating mass destruction."

"What about the Ordinarys, were you able to track them down?"

"We didn't have time. A few Rogues spotted the transport and took interest in it. We captured these three, and the others followed underneath it for several miles outside of the City until we were able to lose them. When we arrived back at the City, we started research immediately. Fortunately, we have discovered that this virus is only transmittable through blood, saliva, and sexual interactions; it is not airborne like the previous virus."

Luke took a deep breath, trying to calm the nerves that were doing jumping jacks just beneath his skin. "What does this have to do with the ORC?"

Aden pointed his finger to the next window. "Your answer is in there."

Luke raised his eyebrow and moved toward it slowly, expecting another Rogue like the last two. The room did hold another Rogue, but this one was much different than the other two. He had yellowed, sunken in eyes and had gone completely bald. His skin was a darker green than Luke had observed on the previous two, and was less wrinkly than the others. But also unlike the other two, he was clothed, wearing the normal white tracksuit that Luke wore at the moment. The Rogue had been reading a book on his bed, but he took notice of Luke and stood, stepping over to the window. He smiled as he moved, revealing two rows of long, sharp teeth.

The Rogue stopped inches from the window and cocked his head, observing Luke in the same way that Luke was observing him. He grinned again and leaned forward.

"Hi," his voice came through speaker on either side of the window.

"Hi," Luke gave an almost breathless response.

Aden came up beside Luke. "We believe that all three of the Rogues we brought in were in different stages of mutation. At first we thought he was one of the newest Rogues, but he has only gotten more intelligent with time, leading us to believe he is one of the *first* to be infected."

"We need to talk," Luke looked at his father.

Aden nodded. "Yes, I think we do."

Chapter Twenty-One

Ally's arms and legs felt as if they weighed a hundred pounds each. She tried to open her mouth and speak, but the darkness she was trapped in filled her lungs before she could utter a sound.

"Ally..."

A voice spoke in the distance, calling to her.

"Ally..."

It was closer this time, beckoning her to wake up. She struggled against the heavy veil over her, managing to raise her hand slightly.

"Ally..."

"I'm here," she managed to whisper, forcing her words free.

"Ally..."

Something sharp pierced her skin and the darkness fled. She found herself bathed in a brilliant, white light, and she could finally open her eyes.

"Ally," Luke stood above her, his hands cupping her face. "Can you hear me?"

She blinked several times, wondering if her mind was playing tricks on her. She had begun to believe that she would be suspended in the darkness for eternity, caught in a silent nightmare.

"Yes," she responded.

Luke leaned forward and gently placed a kiss below each of her eyes. "I've come to take you home."

"Stosh?" she croaked. Her voice was having trouble working after a long period of silence. Either that or it was still raw from her screaming.

"He is waking up now. We are going to bring him home as well," Luke responded.

"How long have I been here?"

"You were brought in yesterday morning, and it is now late afternoon, so over a day."

Luke's face was a shadow with the bright lights positioned directly behind his head, but Ally could almost see his features she knew them so well. His violet eyes, his sometimes crooked smile, and the hard lines of his jaw. She wanted to reach up and touch his face, but she didn't trust her arm to work correctly just yet.

"My mother. Aden—" She forced out.

"I know," Luke rubbed a thumb across her cheek, brushing away a tear she hadn't realized she let escape. "Do you think you can sit up?"

"I can try." She lifted her head slowly, letting him wrap his arm around her back to give her support. Her head still felt foggy, and white dots danced in front of her eyes, but she was eventually able to achieve a sitting position. She dangled her legs over the edge of the table, waiting for the vertigo to pass. Luke stood directly next to her, his body pressed into the side of her leg. He kept one hand on her back and the other on her knee, helping to keep her steady.

"Ally?" She recognized Stosh's voice immediately.

She turned her head slowly, finding him sitting up on the bed next to her. Two female Exceptionals sat on either side of him, acting as his support. Ally fought the urge to jump off her bed and run to him, reminding herself that she was still weakened. Stosh looked her over and then his eyes moved over to Luke, narrowing as he took in the Exceptional who was standing so close to his sister. Ally realized that

Luke had his arm around her shoulder and his free hand on her leg. Of course Stosh would be upset to see that.

"Stosh," she said his name, shooting him a weary smile. "About time you got up."

"You always have to be first, don't you?" he joked back.

"I am older by six minutes," she rebutted. "I started out in first place."

"Where are we? Where is mother?" He rubbed his temples with his fingers. "I can't remember anything after entering that interrogation room."

Luke stiffened beside her, and Ally clutched the edge of the table, feeling dizzy again. She leaned into Luke's chest for support, taking deep breaths. Of course Stosh wouldn't remember what happened to their mother. He had been knocked out cold before Aden had pulled the trigger, and had been asleep since then.

"Ally?" Stosh's voice held an edge of panic. "What happened?"

Somehow, she managed to compose herself. With Luke's help she swiveled on the table and faced her brother, reaching her arm toward him. He did the same, grasping her hand with his own. Tears spilled down her cheeks as she looked up to meet his gaze.

"No... NO!" he yelled, dropping her hand. "Ally, tell me it isn't true."

Ally shook her head. "I'm sorry, Stosh. I'm so sorry."

He leaned back onto the bed, covering his face with his arms. Ally stayed on her own bed, watching as her brother cried into the sleeve of his shirt. She didn't hold him or run her hands through his hair, like her mother would have. She didn't have the strength inside of herself to tell him everything was going to be okay, when she couldn't even convince herself. She couldn't even seem to feel enough emotion to cry along with him. She was numb.

It was dark by the time they left the City Center and made the all too familiar trip to Luke's home. It had taken Ally a good ten minutes to regain proper use of her legs. It took Stosh twenty minutes, and through the process he refused to let Ally or Luke help him. They watched from the edge of the room, seated on metal chairs. She and Stosh washed up and changed into fresh clothes before leaving: Ally in white and Stosh in gray. Several Exceptional Guards escorted them from the building, and Ally didn't manage to catch a glimpse of Aden on their way out. There was so much she wanted to say to him—*do* to him— and she found herself bothered by Luke's dismissive attitude about it. He didn't seem overly upset and was even fairly passive about the whole situation.

Stosh remained emotionless the whole walk to Luke's house, but he couldn't hide his curiosity when they stepped into the foyer. His eyes grew wide and his mouth hung slightly open as he looked around the large room. Ally wondered if she wore a similar expression when she had first arrived. She had barely known what any of the gadgets or objects in the room were until Sabine explained them to her.

Right on cue, Sabine skipped into the room. "You're home!"

How many times had they had a reunion just like this one since Ally's arrival? Especially in the last few days. Asher and Flint followed close behind.

Ally grinned and said, "That line is getting old."

Sabine laughed and hugged her. "Then maybe you should stop leaving."

Ally wished that was a promise she could make, but she had no intention of staying in the City much longer. She had made the decision on their walk home that evening. She couldn't reside in the same City as Aden with out killing him. And killing him was not an option at this time. Some day she would have her revenge for him murdering her mother. For now, she needed to get her friends and family far as far away from him as she could.

"Sabine. Asher. Flint. This is my brother, Stosh." She motioned to Stosh, who stood still beside her. He was done observing the room now, and was instead observing the others.

Sabine blushed as she held out her hand. "Hello."

Stosh took it tentatively. "Hi".

He shook Asher's hand next, followed by Flint, and then crossed his arms over his chest. Stosh was usually outgoing around new people and loved to explore new places, so Ally felt concerned at the withdrawn front he was currently displaying. The five of them stood in awkward silence until Asher finally spoke. "Mazzi saved you some dinner. She said she could either serve you in the kitchen or in your rooms."

Luke took Ally's hand in his. "Why don't you show Stosh around the first floor and get him some dinner. I need to talk to Ally in private."

This was something else that seemed to be on repeat in Ally's life. Luke was constantly rushing her up to his room so they could speak in private. She wondered how that really looked to the others in the house.

"No way. I'm coming with you," Stosh said as he grabbed Ally's other arm. "No way I'm letting you go anywhere with him."

"Stosh," Ally sighed. "I've been here with him for the past month. I can promise you that he isn't going to hurt me. We just need to talk."

Stosh's brows furrowed together. "Yeah, and last time I saw him he told me you were *fine*. But then I find you in the custody of the City leader, our mother is dead, and we spend a day in a half in medically induced comas!"

Ally felt Luke tense up beside her.

Ally's mouth hung open as she turned to face him. "What does he mean *the last time he saw you*."

Luke squeezed his eyes shut. "Ally—"

"Tell me!" she shouted.

"He came—" Stosh started but Ally held up her hand to silence him.

"Luke is right, we need to speak in private. You should go with the others, Stosh," she shot him an apologetic look.

Sabine grabbed Stosh's arm and pulled him backward, somehow convincing him to follow her and Asher into the kitchen.

"Let's talk upstairs," Luke said.

"Gladly." She crossed her arms over her chest and stomped up the stairs, heading straight to Luke's bedroom. He shut the door behind them and turned to face her.

"You have to understand, Ally. I planned on telling you. It was just before the incident at the Warehouse, so you can see why it got pushed aside on my list of priorities."

Ally glared at him. "Why? Why did you go see my brother?"

Luke sighed and rubbed his forehead with his hand. "You used to mumble his name in your sleep, your mother's too. You always seemed so worried about them, and I could only imagine that they felt the same. I went to tell them that you were alive, and doing well despite the circumstance."

"You did?" Ally felt her mood soften. "Thank you."

Luke's violet eyes widened in surprise. "I... well, I wasn't expecting that."

Ally laughed. "I wasn't either. But, really, thank you. I just think it would be better if you didn't lie to protect me so much."

He stepped forward and pulled her into his arms. "Fair enough."

Ally didn't have the heart to tell him that she was feeling so forgiving because of the plans she had. If she wanted any chance of convincing him to leave with her, she would need to play nice. That meant being insensitive to the world around her, and maybe even more insensitive to the feelings she had for Luke.

LUKE FILLED HER IN on his arrival at Aden's office and how he learned of her mother's death. She was pleased to discover that he had thrown Aden at a window out of anger. He then went into how Aden led him to the secret laboratory within the building and he described to Ally what he saw within those walls, ending with the intelligent Rogue he met last.

"Just when we thought Exceptionals couldn't get any more superior," Ally laughed.

"They aren't superior, they are animals," Luke's voice held a defensive tone.

"I thought you said the last one was—is— intelligent?" she asked.

"He is, but he is still a Rogue," he answered.

"This is connected to the ORC, isn't it?" They were seated on the couch in Luke's room, their backs pressed against opposite sides so that they could face each other.

211

"Yes. After we left the laboratory, I sat down and talked with my father about what he had shown me. Apparently, fifteen years ago, before the ORC was first established, a group of scientists were doing research about the dropping population. The scientists were worried that in just a short time, we would no longer be sustainable. Several years later, the same scientists also discovered the potential for our genes to mutate further, but they couldn't say what our bodies would do with the change. With those two things in mind, Aden created the ORC."

Ally hated the way Luke was speaking about his father right now, and about the ORC. He almost sounded as though he supported it, and as though he agreed with everything Aden had done.

Luke continued, "When the Rogues were first discovered, several were captured to run tests. Not only were their genes mutating at an accelerated rate, but also other functions of their bodies were beginning to shut down. Functions that normal Exceptionals already have weakened versions of compared to Ordinarys."

Ally had never heard anyone mention any part of an Exceptional that was weaker than an Ordinary. She didn't think it was a mere coincidence that the information never got out. Exceptionals would never allow themselves to be viewed as less than others.

"Which parts?" Ally asked.

"Exceptionals have trouble conceiving children." he gazed down at his hands while he spoke. "Some are completely sterile, while others can only manage to produce one or two children. The first Exceptionals were able to reproduce with out any issue, but with each generation it gets more difficult. Our bodies are superior, but so much that they are not favorable for bearing children, even Exceptional ones."

Ally let his words play over in her head twice more before

212

speaking. "But the City has always seemed so full."

Luke looked up. "It is a miracle that we have sustained as long as we have. The world had almost reached extinction level when the virus was first released, and there is only one reason we were able to rebuild a sustainable population."

"Ordinarys," Ally answered for him. "With out us, you never would have survived this long."

"With out *them*." Luke looked up. "You're one of us now."

"I've been an Ordinary my whole life, Luke."

He reached up and grabbed something off the bookcase beside the couch. When he handed it to her she realized she was holding a small, hand mirror.

"Take a look," he said.

She held the mirror up slowly, staring at the reflection of her own face. She fought the urge to gasp, not wanting to look overly surprised at what she saw. Her eyes were almost completely violet, with just a few dots of green shining through. The lines of her face were sharper, and more defined, and even her skin had a shimmery quality to it. No wonder Stosh had trouble looking at her.

"Enough distractions." She threw the mirror to the ground. "So Aden thinks the ORC will not only continue to keep the population up, but also help with this Rogue issue?"

"Essentially," Luke continued. "He knew two things when he started the ORC. One, Ordinary women could bear children very easily, and at least twice as many as Exceptionals. And two, all children that had at least one Exceptional parent would be Exceptional as well."

"Except for my brother," Ally added.

Luke nodded. "That would be a first."

"And the Rogue situation?"

"The ORC has become a way not only to raise a sustainable population, but also to raise our numbers in case of a war. Species will always try to survive and once the Rogues run out of resources in the Eastern City, they'll begin to move west."

"That's terrifying," Ally said. She tried to imagine Rogues infiltrating her own settlement, biting and scratching Ordinarys. She tried to imagine herself, Luke, and the other Exceptionals changing into the horrible monsters Luke had described to her. "Aden is building himself a mini army."

"He has tried to keep our numbers above theirs, especially with the Exceptionals."

"Wouldn't it take several generations to build up the population?" Ally didn't know much about science and numbers, but it didn't seem like ten years would have a large effect on the current population, considering the small amount of volunteers they were bringing in."

"That was the plan," Luke responded. "But then the Rogues came along."

"Why force the Ordinarys into the breeding program? Why not explain the situation?"

Luke cocked his head. "Do you think they would have believed Aden, especially with the image they have of him outside the City? He didn't want to create mass panic in the settlements, and he certainly didn't want anyone to travel east to see if the Rogues were really there. Could you imagine if an Ordinary somehow escaped their grasp and led a group of them back here?"

"It would be awful," she responded, one of her eyebrows arching toward the ceiling. "And are you really attempting to justify the ORC?"

"I'm not." Luke reached out and took her hand. "I'm trying to show you a different point of view. Everything being done right now, is being done to ensure the safety of the City. We need numbers, and now we have them."

"Yes, of children. And what about all of these children, does Aden plan to make them fight for the City?"

"Aden doesn't expect the Rogues to make a move toward our City any time soon, he just knows that they will. It could be in five years, ten years, or even twenty years. By then, we'll be ready for them."

"How are we prepared? No one knows about this."

"Everyone will know, and soon. I'm making sure of that," Luke said, leaning forward. "Aden has been training twice the normal amount of Guards for the City."

"What about all of the Ordinarys in the settlements? How will they prepare?" she asked.

"Aden has a plan for that as well," he said. "He is having a shelter built north of the City. It is a full day's journey away, and far enough that he believes everyone will be safe."

"Why are you putting so much faith in him now?" Ally leaned toward him, their bodies only a foot apart now. "What if he is making this all up? You have never trusted him before."

"I saw the Rogues with my own eyes, Ally. You didn't. And because if I ignore him, and he happens to be right… I'll never be able to forgive myself."

"These Rogues, do they have powers like yours? Are they as strong?" Questions flew through her mind as she tried to process all of the new information she was receiving.

"Yes, they have retained their abilities from when they were Exceptionals. Their powers are not as controlled though. Through the animalistic stage, they lost the inner sense of what they could do. It was as though they had to start over, and retrain themselves to use their abilities. They are physically stronger as well. Aden said it is as though twice the adrenaline courses through their bodies. They can jump higher, lift heavier objects, and run faster."

Ally had seen Exceptional Guards move through the woods at a dizzying pace, their bodies almost a blur as they ran. She couldn't imagine the Rogues, whose appearances sounded extra frightening, moving through the woods at an even faster rate.

"We need to tell the others," she stood and straightened her clothes. "They need to know."

Luke jumped up and grabbed her arm. "We can't, Ally. I promised my father. I shouldn't even be telling you, but he knew he could never control that."

"You said everyone would know soon enough, so why not now?"

"The information needs to be given in a proper way. If you tell the others, and they let it slip, the news will travel through the City by way of gossip. There is a good chance there will be widespread panic."

"I think there will be widespread panic either way," Ally said.

Luke nodded. "I'm not saying there won't be, but Aden needs a chance to deliver the message with the best information he can give."

A bell chimed, signaling that their dinner had arrived through the chute in Luke's room. He left Ally's side and went over to grab the trays, setting them up on the table in the corner. As she watched him, she couldn't help but finally feel the panic that was rising up within her. Deep down, she had a feeling everything Aden had told Luke about the

Rogues was true, but she still had trouble trusting him. Aden had killed her mother, and with out cause. He couldn't have the best interest of others in mind; the only person that mattered in his mind was himself. It scared her that Luke trusted him so easily now. All of this information was even more reason for Ally to take the others and leave the City with them, and soon.

Ally didn't bother leaving Luke's room that night. She couldn't face Stosh or her friends knowing what she knew, and not being able to tell them. She took a shower until the hot water ran cold, and then stood under the water for several more minutes. Luke finally had to come in and drag her out and she couldn't even feel embarrassed that he saw her undressed. He wrapped her in several towels while her teeth chattered from the cold, her body attempting to warm itself up. Exceptionals didn't feel extreme temperatures like an Ordinary did, which was a further sign that her body was still going through the changing process.

It wasn't until she was dressed and in bed, wrapped in the warmth of Luke's embrace, that she finally broke down and allowed herself to cry. She cried for her mother. She cried for Stosh. She cried for the Ordinarys still in the ORC. She cried for the life she had lost, and the uncertainty of her future. Tears spilled out of her eyes and onto Luke's shirt, and he held her tightly until she cried herself to sleep, silently willing the nightmares to stay away.

And they did.

Chapter Twenty-Two

When she woke up the next morning, she was still cradled in Luke's embrace. Her face felt stiff from the tears that had dried on her cheeks, and she could already tell that her eyes were puffy. She leaned her head up toward Luke's and found that he was awake, watching her carefully.

"You must think I'm insane," she said with a small laugh.

"Nah." He smiled, but his eyes remained cautious. "I think you care a lot about your friends and family, and would do anything to see them safe. I may not show it in a similar way, but I'm just as terrified as you. All I've been able to think about is how I am going to keep you safe. I haven't done such a good job so far."

Ally smiled. "You saved me that day in the woods, when we first met. With out you, who knows where I would be right now, or what I would be doing."

This time he leaned forward to kiss her and their mouths met. They lay that way for a while, ignoring the constant buzzes from the kitchen announcing that breakfast was ready. Ally felt a distant need to push Luke away, but found that she could find the will to do so. Finally, Sabine knocked loudly on the door, saying that if they didn't come out, Stosh was threatening to come in.

"Stosh," Ally pulled back from Luke, sitting up. "I almost forgot that he is here. I think somewhere inside; I was hoping it was a nightmare. That he was home and safe, in the settlement."

"Right now, inside the City might be the safest place for him."

Luke pointed out, sitting up next to her.

She ignored him, jumping out of bed and running her hand through her hair. She had slept in Luke's room before, and in the same bed as him, but something about her brother knowing this scared her. She had never dated anyone back in the settlement, so she had never seen that protective side of him. She had no idea how he would react when he saw her, or what he was thinking right now. And truthfully, she felt awful for spending the night in Luke's bed, knowing that she was leaving him. Last night she had made the decision to be less sensitive to her feelings for Luke, and look how easily she had fallen into a morning of kissing him.

When Ally, Luke, and Sabine stepped into the kitchen, they found Asher, Flint, and Stosh all gathered around the table, shoving food into their mouths. Stosh actually had a smile on his face, and laughed at something one of the boys had said. Ally stepped toward the table hesitantly.

"Hey," she said.

Stosh looked up and smiled, but it didn't quite reach his eyes. "Hey Al. The food here is amazing."

He shoved another spoonful of scrambled eggs into his mouth.

"Can we talk?" she asked, motioning toward the doors that led to the back garden.

He nodded, pushing his plate back and standing up. Luke stepped beside her but she told him to stay, leading just Stosh out onto the patio. She kept walking until she found her way to the fountain and the bench she had begun to call her own. After they were seated she took Stosh's hand, cupping it the way she used to when they were much younger.

"You've changed." Stosh spoke first, still not meeting her gaze.

"Stosh, look at me," she said, waiting until he raised his head and their eyes met. "I might look different, but I'm still the same Ally."

Stosh shook his head. "It isn't just your looks. You are becoming more like *them* in demeanor as well." He pointed toward the house.

"There is no *them* for me anymore, Stosh." She thought back to her reflection in the mirror last night. She had to come to terms with what she was becoming. "I'm an Exceptional now."

"What's that mean for us?" he asked.

She looked at the fountain, which was turned off at the moment. "I don't see why it has to mean anything. You'll always be my twin brother, Stosh."

"Will they let me go home? I'm not sure I want to stay here."

Ally frowned. "I can't answer that, but I am guessing it will be quite the fight to send you home. There is a reason that Ordinarys never return from the City."

Ally filled him in on her time in the City so far. She told him about her arrival and getting to know Luke and the others. She tried to paint the picture as brightly as she could, so he could see how wonderful people here really could be, Exceptionals and Ordinarys alike. It was harder to fill him in on the breeding center, and he grew visibly angered when she talked about her time there. She told him about how she ended up at the Warehouse, and how she found out that she was an Exceptional. Their journeys collided the following day in Aden's office.

Stosh listened intently, managing to hold her gaze. "I'm just glad you're alive. I spent weeks wondered what had happened to you after the Guards had taken you, and then Luke showed up. As much as I

220

hate to admit it, I can tell that guy really cares about you."

Ally smiled. "I care about him, too."

Stosh rolled his eyes. "Can we change the subject before I lose my breakfast?"

"What have *you* been doing, back in the settlement?" Ally asked, having been curious about this her whole time here.

Stosh leaned back and looked up at the cloudless sky. "That day that you were taken, I ran all the way back to the settlement. By the time I arrived I was so out of breath, and so upset, it took me almost thirty minutes to start explaining what had happened. Of course, there was nothing we could do. It was just like when they come for volunteers, being brought into the City is final. I thought they would all be angry with me for leaving you, but life went back to normal, as if you had chosen to go instead of being captured. Mother and I mourned in private that night, realizing that we would never see you again."

"We had to continue on with our lives. We still did our daily work and joined in the required settlement activities, but nothing was enjoyable. I stopped going out with our friends, thinking that if you couldn't be there to enjoy it, I shouldn't either. Almost every afternoon, I went back to the boundary line, saying that I would jump it for you. Each day I tried, but I just couldn't do it. I couldn't do the very thing that made me lose you. A few times I contemplated marching across the creek and into Exceptional territory, hoping that they would take me inside and I could rescue you, but I knew I couldn't leave mother alone. She was so broken after you left, losing me too would have killed her."

He choked out the last words, a single tear rolling down his cheek. Ally felt tears roll down her own cheeks and she slipped an arm around Stosh, leaning her head on his shoulder. "At the beginning of my time here, I kept asking myself why I had to jump the boundary line that day. If I had just stayed back, like you wanted to, then I would still be in the settlement with you and Mother. Right now, she would still be alive. But good things *have* happened to me while I've been here, so I cannot completely regret it."

"Good things like Luke?" Stosh pulled back from her.

"Yes, like Luke," she said.

"You know, I don't trust him, because of who his father is."

Ally nodded her head slightly. "I can understand that. I'm just asking you to give him a chance."

They stared at the fountain for a little while longer, neither of them speaking. Eventually they found their way back into the house and Stosh headed off on a house tour led by Sabine, Asher, and Flint. Luke stayed behind and waited with Ally, taking her hand in his.

"What happens now?" she asked.

"We head to the Institute, where you'll begin your training. It was one of Aden's requirements for me taking you home so early. He trusts me more now, and I need to keep my word."

Ally didn't like the idea of going to the Institute. It took her further from the boundary wall, and further from her plan of escaping. But she needed to do this for Luke right now, and she couldn't help but be curious about her own abilities. If there was any chance that they could help her once she was outside of the City, then she needed to learn how to use them properly.

The walk to the Institute felt different than before. Instead of shrinking into the crowd and keeping her eyes focused on her feet, she walked with her head held high. She was an Exceptional now, and she needed to start acting like one. Luke held her hand, leading her through the streets. A few Exceptionals recognized her from the Warehouse and stopped to say hello. Others whispered to each other while they watched her pass, giving Ally a sinking feeling about what they might be saying.

Pax met them in the Institute lobby and gave Ally a hug, startling her. "Welcome to the group."

Luke laughed. "Don't scare her out of it Pax."

Pax backed up, still grinning. "Ready for your first day of training?"

Ally didn't know much about Luke's friends, but Pax seemed kind enough. Despite being in training to become an Exceptional Guard, he was always smiling and paid her some attention when she was around. She smiled back, trying not to grow too attached. She wouldn't be around him for long.

"As ready as I can be," she responded.

"I'll take you to the training center. We have practice for the graduation ceremony today," Luke said as he pulled her away from Pax.

"Ceremony?" Ally raised an eyebrow.

"They put us in these black robes and make us listen to a speech from my father. It signifies our passing from teenage Exceptionals to adults. It officially gives us the right to move into our career training, and if you are a guy, grow your hair out." Luke rubbed his hand through his short hair.

Ally laughed. "I don't know if I can picture you with anymore hair than that."

"It's been buzzed my whole life, so I am right there with you." He led her down a main hall to the right and into the elevator. They went down several flights before the machine stopped and they exited into another hall.

"I wish I could stay with you," Luke said, turning around to face her.

"I wish you could too, but even if you didn't have anywhere to be, this is probably something I need to do on my own. I need to know that I can handle this." She leaned forward and kissed him. "I'll see you at lunch?"

He nodded. "I'll see you then."

He stepped back into the elevator and Ally watched him until the doors closed. She followed the hall to a large, open room. Several other Exceptionals were there working with their own abilities, and she tried to picture Luke in this very room, practicing along with them.

A female Exceptional came up from behind her. "You must be Ally. I'm Dr. Loo. Shall we get started?"

The doctor wore a long, white lab coat, marking her position in the City. She was shorter than Ally, which was surprising for an Exceptional, and had a round face and almond shaped eyes, like Maver. Ally shook away memories of the doctors from the ORC, and from Aden's office, and tried to focus on the task she was being handed today. She needed to get a better grasp of her abilities and what they were.

Dr. Loo led her into a small room off to the side of the main training area. "We'll first need to get an idea of what you can do now, so we can assess and decide what you might be able to do in the future."

Ally looked down at her hands. "I'm not sure that I *can* do anything now. I've only used my abilities twice, and both times I was extremely angry and very upset."

Dr. Loo tapped her fingers along her porta-comp, making notes. "I want you to close your eyes."

Ally did as she asked, spacing her legs apart for balance.

Dr. Loo continued, "Search within yourself for the energy that binds your abilities. Feel for the buzzing it creates in you, that vibrating force it puts off."

Ally did as Dr. Loo asked, even though she thought she would be unsuccessful. She had no idea how she would find that inner energy without something making her mad first. Right now she only felt frustrated that she couldn't display any sort of ability, like the other Exceptionals. She was about to tell Dr. Loo that it was hopeless when she felt it. It buzzed beneath her ribs, pulsing with her heart rate. She kept her eyes closed and tried to focus on the energy, finding that she could almost feel it, as though she were touching it with her hands. There it was; a small orb of light floating at the center of her being.

"I have it," she managed to croak out.

"Good!" Dr. Loo sounded pleased. "Now help it expand. Imagine it growing until it travels upward and into your arms.

Again, Ally did as she was asked, and was surprised at how quickly the energy responded to her thoughts. She could feel, as well as see, it moving upward and through her body. The vibrating energy filled her completely, and she could feel her control over it. She opened her eyes, knowing she could still keep focus of it.

Dr. Loo was smiling. "Now, we know that you can blast objects backwards, which tells us you can probably move them around as well."

She took a red rubber ball from a bin in the corner of the room and placed it on the floor between them. "I want you to raise this ball off the floor, and move it back to the bin."

Ally nodded and focused on the ball, raising her arms like she had seen others do, and like she had done when she used her abilities before. Her fingers tingled from the energy and she looked at the ball,

225

imaging it moving across the room. A bright light burst from her palms, and the energy escaped her almost all at once. She quickly gained control of it, pulling her hands back to her body.

Dr. Loo had jumped to the back wall, an amused look on her face. "Usually we are trying to increase the output of energy in Exceptionals, but for you, we are going to need to work on holding it in until we see what you can do."

Ally stared at the spot where the ball had been just moments before. Shards of red rubber were scattered around a black scorch mark in the floor.

"I'm sorry," she whispered.

"Don't apologize. You aren't the first Exceptional to destroy a training tool, and you won't be the last. This is why you are here Ally, so that we can work on your abilities. We can't have you running around the City with an unknown power. We want to help you contain it, and control it, so you don't pose a danger to yourself or anyone else."

Ally nodded. "Let's do it again."

Dr. Loo grabbed another red ball from the bin. "I have at least a dozen more of these in there."

"Bring it on," Ally said.

Chapter Twenty-Three

Luke waited anxiously in the lunchroom, hoping Ally would arrive soon. He had been nervous to leave her down in the training center, knowing just how overwhelming it could be at first. He hoped she was having success with whichever trainer they paired her with, and that she hadn't injured herself or anyone else in the process.

Maver walked up to the table, a tray in his hand. "I know you're eating with Ally today, but I need to tell you something. I went to the ORC, like you asked, and looked for the Ordinary you mentioned."

"And?" Luke sat up straighter, intent on listening to Maver's information.

"They said she had been moved to one of the housing units," he responded. "And I think you know what that means."

Luke kicked the leg of the table. "She's pregnant."

"I tried," Maver shrugged his shoulders.

"I know, and I appreciate it." Ally walked into the lunchroom just then, looking around for him. "Hey, we'll talk more later."

He stood and waved to Ally, who had finally noticed him. She had an intense look on her face, and she strode across the cafeteria with heavy steps. He kept the grin on his face, hopeful that she would have something good to report, and pulled her into his arms when she drew close enough.

"How did it go?" he asked.

She pulled back and looked thoughtful for a minute. "Do you want the good or the bad?"

"The good."

She smiled. "I was able to move two red balls across the room with out touching them."

"That's good," he responded, knowing that there was more coming.

"But I moved them so quickly that they shot through the walls and into the training area. One took out two male Exceptionals that were practicing with fire."

Luke stifled a laugh. "They probably needed a strike to their egos."

"And that isn't even mentioning the ten balls I managed to explode right on the spot before achieving moving just *one*," she added.

He took her hand and led her to the lunch line. "Any progress is good at this point. What did you think of your trainer?"

"She's nice." Ally grabbed a clean tray from the stack. "It is all very interesting. I am just trying to be patient with my abilities. I want them to be controlled *now*. I want to understand them *now*."

Luke knew exactly how she felt. He had had the same thoughts in his first few days at the training center. "It will come, and hopefully fast. You've adapted so well already, I'm sure you'll have this down in no time."

Once they were seated at a table Ally changed the subject. "How did your ceremony practice go?"

"It was boring." He leaned forward and whispered, "My father decided to make the announcement at the ceremony, since most of the City attends."

Ally's eyes grew wide. "Wait, and it's tomorrow?"

Luke nodded. "He is taking this all very seriously, which I am glad to see. Hopefully with enough preparation, we can be prepared for whenever the Rogues decide to make a move."

"You know, I was thinking. Remember those movies you showed me, the ones with the wars back before the virus," she asked.

Luke nodded, recalling several movies he owned that fit that description. He wasn't sure exactly which one Ally was talking about, but they all held a similar theme. Countries used to fight over things like fuel, land, and even money. They went to war and sometimes almost completely annihilated each other, killing thousands of innocent people with guns and bombs.

Ally continued, "What about those explosives that were used to take out large cities or towns? Couldn't Aden just take them all out at once?"

Luke was surprised by her suggestion. "We've never replicated the bombs shown in those movies. The early Exceptionals decided that it would be a disservice to our country to waste time on building them. The world had already experienced enough destruction. They wanted to focus on rebuilding, not continuing to bring each other down. They decided that guns would hold enough protection. No one would be going to war anytime soon."

"Until now." Ally took a bite of her sandwich. "We could actually use them now."

"Not exactly." Luke played with his napkin. "Aden mentioned capturing the Rogues and putting them into some sort of rehabilitation program. He wants to study them further, and see if there is anything we can do to reverse the process."

"Like the vaccine for SS-16," Ally said. "The vaccine that has kept me an Ordinary all this time."

Luke nodded. "Yes. It would be a waste of life to kill all of those Rogues, and would result in backward progress in raising the population. We are talking hundreds of thousands of lives. If there is any hope of them being saved, we need to at least try. Aden still holds on to the City founders' dreams that we would one day rebuild the country to something close to what it was before."

Ally smirked. "If he really wanted that, then he would be passing out vaccines to all of the remaining Exceptionals."

Luke crumbled his napkin into a ball. "I don't want to argue about this again."

"No wonder Aden was so interested in it." Ally completely ignored him. "I wonder if it will work on curing the Rogues."

Luke had talked to his father about this very thing just two days ago. "That has been put into consideration. They'll never know until they find the man you told them about. They are still searching the Wilderness."

Ally smiled as he finished his sentence, and something about the motion worried Luke. Had Ally lied to his father about the location of the Ordinary with the vaccine? He didn't blame her, considering the position she had been placed in, but now would be a good time to step forward with the real location. If it would help cure the Rogues, it would save them a lot of trouble, and possibly save their lives.

They spent the rest of their lunch talking more about the ceremony and what it would entail. Ally would have the day off from training and classes, and would be able to attend to watch. Before she headed back down to the training area, they planned to meet in the lobby at the end of the afternoon and walk home together. Ally was already changing so much since she had discovered her Exceptional abilities, and Luke hoped that it didn't push her any further from him than she was already starting to feel.

LATER THAT DAY, Luke met Ally in the lobby just like they had discussed.

"I want to take you somewhere before we go home," he said as she came up beside him.

"Where?" she asked, taking his hand. The gesture brightened his mood.

"It's a surprise," he said, leading her away from the Institute.

It didn't take long for them to arrive at their destination. He had brought her back to the park he had taken her to on her first day out of the house. Here he had answered her questions about the City, and tried to make her feel more comfortable with him. That day, he knew that she was special, but he had no idea just how much she would come to mean to him.

Ally smiled and walked over to the large oak tree in the middle of the grassy area. She pulled back her shirtsleeve and looked at her forearm, glancing back and forth between the tree and where her mark used to be.

Luke stepped up beside her. "Your mark?"

She nodded. "It's strange, but I kind of miss it."

He ran his hand along the spot where her mark had once been. She turned and sat down, falling backward into the grass. "I was wondering if we would ever come back to this place. It feels like years since we laid here last, when in reality it was just under a month ago."

Luke joined her on the ground, resting on his side so that he could look at her. "You were so timid around me, and scared."

She laughed. "Could you blame me?"

"Not really," he smiled. "But you've changed entirely."

"Think of it more as getting to know the real me. The girl I was back in the settlement," she said. "I think you have as well, changed that is."

"What do you mean?" he asked.

"You seem different these days," she shrugged.

Luke took a deep breath. "I need to ask you something important. But first, I need to tell you something important."

Ally closed her eyes. "Hold on, give me a minute to decipher that."

He laughed, lifting his hand and running his fingers along her cheek gently.

"Ally... I love you."

Her eyes popped open. "What?" She sat up slowly, turning to face him. "What did you say?"

"I love you. And I mean it." She started to respond but he held his finger up to her mouth. "You don't have to say anything back, I just needed you to know. I know we haven't known each other very long, but I can't deny how I feel about you."

"What were you going to ask me?" Her voice cracked, and her cheeks were reddening with embarrassment.

"Are you going to leave me?"

She looked at the ground immediately, suddenly finding her shoes very interesting. He cursed and fell back onto the ground, covering his eyes with his arm. He felt her hand gently touch his arm.

"I want you to come with me. I plan on leaving the City, but

I've never planned on leaving you." He could tell by her voice that she was struggling not to cry.

He lifted his arms and looked at her. "You know I can't do that."

"Why not?" she asked. "Come to the Wilderness with us. We don't need the City, or the people here. You say Aden has this Rogue situation under control, so let him handle it. We can head south, to the old City. I'm sure we could find a place to stay there, to start over. We can keep away from the Rogues."

He was surprised she even knew about the Southern City, but the Ordinarys had a way of holding on to their history.

"Ally." He could hear the pain in his own voice. "I can't. I have to stay and help. I promised my father I would support him in this, and help him. I can't leave the City knowing that everyone here is in harm's way."

"And I can't stay here. I need to leave, with Stosh and Willow, and maybe the others. I need to be with my other family, the Ordinarys in the Settlement. I need to warn them and get them to leave, in case Aden's plans fall apart."

Luke sat up and sighed. They both felt similar loyalties to their own friends and family, and they both felt driven to protect.

"When?" He stared ahead of him, watching as a bird swooped down and ate crumbs from underneath one of the benches.

"Tomorrow."

"So soon?" He jumped up. "Why tomorrow?"

She stood as well, brushing off her pants. "Because of the ceremony. Doesn't it make the most sense? To leave when almost everyone in the City is away from the boundary wall."

"What about the Guards? What is your plan?" Luke stepped toward her but she backed away.

"I can't tell you. I can't risk you getting in the way." She crossed her arms over her chest. "I shouldn't have even told you the when."

"I want to help you, Ally," he said, feeling hurt by her words.

"You've done plenty to help me. Now you just need to let me go." She turned away from him and started to run, leaving the park and disappearing behind one of the houses nearby.

Luke sank onto the ground below, letting everything that just happened wash over him. He had already decided that he would never let Ally go again, but now she was begging him to. She was planning on leaving the City, and he was confident that she would see it through. Now he just needed to decide whether or not he would be going with her?

Chapter Twenty-Four

Ally sprinted the whole way back to Luke's house, not tiring at all. He had told her that he loved her. *Loved.* It wasn't a word that she expected to hear come from his mouth so soon, but as he spoke it, she could feel the truth behind it. She could also sense from her own being that maybe she felt the same as well. She burst into the foyer and immediately searched out Stosh, Sabine, Asher, and Flint. She found the four of them in the dining room, polishing the expensive plates from the display case.

Stosh looked up from an intricately designed cup he was holding. "Hey. Have you seen these things called movies they have here? Amazing!"

Ally contained her laugh, trying to remain focused. "Are Aden or Luke's mom here?"

Sabine shook her head. "It's just us right now."

"Good." She sat down and took a plate and a rag, joining in on their polishing party. "We are going to leave the City tonight."

Sabine dropped the cup she was holding, managing to grab it just before it hit the table. "What?"

"You heard me," Ally said. "Everyone is preparing for the graduation ceremony tomorrow, so the regular Exceptionals will be busy. On top of that, I figure the Guards will almost expect an escape of some sort tomorrow, so they will probably be lax about their security tonight."

She didn't mention how she had told Luke that she was leaving tomorrow, and didn't want him to mess with their plans. Especially now that he had told her he loved her. It would be that much harder for her to leave him behind and she needed to make this decision quickly.

"You mean we are going home?" Stosh perked up, setting the cup on the table. "I'm in, tell me what I need to do."

Sabine's head shot toward Stosh, her cheeks turning a bright pink. "I guess I'm in too."

"I have a plan, but first we need to find Willow," Ally said.

"Willow is here?" Stosh sat forward. "You didn't tell me that."

When Ally had told him about her time at the ORC, she had left the part about Willow out, not wanting to upset him further.

Now she gave him all the details and finished with, "We need to find her first, and then we can go. I can't leave her behind."

The five of them finally agreed on what they would do and went their separate ways to prepare for the trip. Ally was beginning to think that Luke would never come back to the house, and that would mess up her plan entirely. She was actually surprised that it took him as long as it did. She thought he would have come after her almost immediately, but it took him over an hour to show up. She was, however, able to predict that he would want to speak with her privately, and it was something she had been counting on.

She paced in the middle of his room. "I need to know where Willow is. Have you found her yet?"

Luke nodded. "Maver informed me just before you arrived at lunch today. Just in time for your escape it seems."

She could hear the contempt in his voice but she ignored it. "Where is she?"

"She is back with the ORC," he responded.

Ally tried not to let that information phase her. "So Coarse is finished with her. Could you go there tonight and request to have her?"

Luke shook his head. "For starters, we cannot take more than one Ordinary from the ORC at a time. If we win their contract at the Warehouse, well that is a different story. But, it seems as though Willow is not available for contract at all."

Ally paused for a moment, thinking over his words. When they finally made sense to her, she walked to the bed and sat down. "Willow is pregnant."

He came and sat alongside her, taking her hand. "Yes."

"How will I get her out?" She looked over at him, having trouble making eye contact with him after their talk in the park.

Luke smiled. "This is where I can give you some good news. If an Ordinary is pregnant, and sent to live in the ORC until she has the baby, she is placed in Exceptional housing. Willow will be in one of four housing units surrounding the ORC, and she should be easy to retrieve."

Ally breathed a sigh of relief. "Thank you, Luke, for your help."

He leaned in to kiss her but she pushed him away. They had already resigned to part ways, and she didn't want to give herself any possible reason to stay. He put his head in his hands and turned to look at her.

"I need you to let me help you, Ally. Whatever you have planned, I can help you leave the City safely. I can't stand the thought that something might happen to you while I'm at the ceremony tomorrow. And my father will notice if I'm missing."

Ally groaned and leaned back on the bed. "We are leaving tonight."

The words left her mouth in a rush.

"I assumed that." He laughed but it contained no humor. "You are such a bad liar. I just wanted to see if you would tell me."

She punched his arm. "Not funny. So, what are we going to do first?"

"First, we're going to go get Willow." He stood and offered her his hand, pulling her up.

She had told the others to pack and meet in Sabine's room, which was where Ally and Luke found them.

"Is he coming too?" Stosh asked when Luke stepped into the room.

Ally shook her head. "No, but he is going to help us escape."

Sabine frowned and Asher and Flint looked surprised.

"Did you find out where Willow is?" Sabine stepped forward. Somehow she had found all of them entirely black outfits, just like the ones Ally and Stosh wore back in the settlement.

"Yes, and we'll need to leave as soon as we get her. It won't be long before they notice her absence," Luke answered.

Sabine gave Ally and Luke their own black outfits and they changed quickly, grabbing the packs that Asher held out to them.

"It has enough food and clothing for one week, just in case." He said. They had talked about possibly having to hide out in the woods for a little while until they could get a message back to the settlement. They didn't know just how quickly the Guards would come after them, if they even did.

It was nearing the end of summer, but the sky was still light well into the evening. They waited until the sun disappeared behind the houses and the light outside dimmed considerably. Mazzi saw them off, tears brimming in her eyes. Ally tried to convince her to come with them, but Mazzi said that she felt at home here in the City, even though

238

she wasn't an Exceptional. Ally didn't probe further; everyone needed to make his or her own decision.

Luke led them through side streets and alleys all the way to the ORC. It loomed up ahead of them, drawing memories back into Ally's mind.

"I really hate this place," she whispered.

"There are the housing units." Luke pointed to four large homes. Two sat on the left of the ORC, and two on the right. "I'll take Asher to the homes on the right. Ally, you take Stosh with you to the homes on the left. Sabine and Flint can keep watch."

They all agreed and took their positions. Ally and Stosh hurried across the road and into the alley beside the two housing units. She took a quick peek around the corner so see if Luke and Asher had made it to the other units, but she could no longer see them.

"What is the plan now?" Stosh whispered. "How do we get inside to look for her?"

"We might not need to," Ally whispered in response, pointing to a large window on the first floor. It appeared that both housing units had been designed identically. Bright lights spilled out of the windows and onto the concrete below, creating yellow squares across the small backyard. "It wouldn't be time to turn in just yet, so maybe they are all gathered downstairs. I bet those windows look right into the main room of the home."

They decided it was worth a try and ducked along the back of the house, slowly creeping up to the bottom of the window. Ally motioned for Stosh to move to the next house while she checked this one. Once he had disappeared from her view, she lifted her head slowly and peered into the window. She had been right; it gave a view of the main area of the home. A dozen or so Ordinary girls were scattered through out the room. A few of them were reading books, but the majority of them were watching a movie on a large TV. She looked them all over and didn't see Willow, but she knew that that didn't mean she wasn't in there. Willow could easily be in another room.

"Ally," Stosh popped up beside her and she had to cover her mouth to keep from screaming.

"Don't do that." She slapped him, watching him stifle a laugh.

"I found her," he said with wide eyes, pointing to the housing unit next to the one she had been searching.

They crouched down and moved fast, stopping below the wide window at the back of the unit. She stood up slowly, observing a scene similar to the one she saw in the previous home. Ally found Willow almost immediately. She was seated on a sofa, reading a book and looking extremely bored.

"Did you find her?" Luke came up behind Ally, causing her to shriek into her hand.

"What is with you guys tonight?" She punched Stosh again, who was really having trouble stifling a laugh this time.

"Hey, he did it, not me." Stosh pointed at Luke.

Ally narrowed her eyes at him before looking at Luke. "She is in this one."

"We have an idea to get her out," Luke said. "But you aren't going to like it."

"Oh, well that has me convinced," she responded. "Tell me, what exactly is your idea?"

Flint stepped from the shadows. "I'm going to create a diversion so that you can grab her and get away."

Ally frowned. "What do you mean?"

Stosh placed a hand on her shoulder. "He is going to stay behind, Ally."

She shook her head. "No, we'll think of a different plan so that you can come with us."

Flint gave her a slight smile. "It's okay, Ally, really. I'm like Mazzi; I think I'll be just fine here. I agreed to come along because I didn't want to be left behind, but the Wilderness doesn't sound like the place for me."

Ally looked him over. She hadn't gotten to know him very well in her time here, but he had always been kind to her. She leaned forward and gave him a hug.

"Thank you," she said in his ear before pulling away.

He nodded and stepped away, disappearing around the side of the house.

"What do you think he is going to do?" she asked.

Luke looked into the window. "I'm not sure, but we better act fast once he decides. Which one is Willow?"

Ally pointed her out and he grinned. "She's pretty."

She elbowed him in the side. "Watch it."

They only had to wait a few minutes for Flint's diversion. A loud crash came from the front of the house and they could hear voices yelling from inside. Several of the girls even stood and ran toward the source of the crash. Willow stayed seated but put her book down, looking in the direction of the action.

"Now or never," Luke said, raising his hands. "Everyone duck."

They did as he said and soon glass was raining down on their heads. Luke had somehow blown the back window out and was now

241

jumping up and into the house. Ally followed after him, knowing she didn't need to tell Stosh and Asher to stay behind. Ordinarys couldn't jump that high with that much ease.

The few girls that remained in the room stared at them in horror; a few of them were poised to start screaming. Luke grabbed Willow from the couch and threw her over his shoulder. Ally walked backward behind him, watching the girls.

"Please, you didn't see any of this," she spoke to them.

She jumped back out the window, where Luke was already waiting with the others, Willow still thrown over his shoulder.

"I think she is still drugged," Luke said. "I'll have to carry her to the boundary wall."

Ally didn't question his decision and they all took off in a run back to where Sabine was still waiting. The found her huddled in the corner, tears running down her cheeks from the anticipation. Stosh came to her side and helped her up, whispering something in her ear to settle her down. Ally noticed that Stosh didn't let go of Sabine's hand as they ran, and despite the situation they were currently in, Ally managed to smile.

Luke had told them before they left that he would need to lead them through the back streets to get to their escape point at the boundary wall. Even past dark, the streets would be full of Exceptionals planning for tomorrow's ceremony. They would look especially suspicious with Luke carrying Willow over his shoulder. Ally was losing patience with all the extra time it was taking, knowing that the Guards would be after them soon.

By the time they finally reached the wall, the Ordinarys were having trouble keeping up. Ally was still amazed by her newfound endurance, and had almost forgotten that the others would tire out after a certain distance. This thought added more doubt to the success of their escape once they were out in the woods, and then into the Wilderness. She had no idea how she would hide the others if this happened. She couldn't carry them all.

Stosh stared up at the wall, which rose two stories above them. "How are we going to get over it?"

"Now that we have Luke, it won't be that difficult," Ally smiled.

Luke set Willow down carefully. "I can lift you up one by one and set you on the other side."

Stosh laughed. "Yeah. Right."

Ally had forgotten that this world was new to Stosh. He didn't know about Luke's extra abilities yet.

Luke smirked and flicked his hand, causing Stosh to fall backwards.

"Be nice," she said through gritted teeth.

Stosh stood up quickly, brushing dirt from his shoulder. "Okay okay, I believe you."

Luke shrugged and looked at the wall. "I'll need to scale it first and get to the top, otherwise I won't be able to see you to the other side."

"Let me lift you," Ally suggested.

He looked skeptical. "The girl who made ten rubber balls explodes?"

She touched his arm lightly. "I can do this, I promise. I don't think any part of me, even the one that controls my abilities, could ever hurt you."

Luke seemed to struggle with that thought before finally saying, "Alright, I trust you."

Ally had the others step back while Luke approached the wall. She closed her eyes and reached into her mind, searching for the energy she had been practicing with all afternoon. She found it quickly and made it expand, feeling the familiar tingle in her arms. She opened her eyes and focused on Luke, picturing his safe arrival at the top of the wall. Ever so slightly, she released the power from her hands. Luke shot up quickly and she pulled the energy back, stopping him in mid-air.

"Careful," he warned.

She took a deep breath and nodded. "I can do this."

She started again, managing to release less energy this time. Slowly, Luke began to rise toward the top of the wall. He was currently sideways in the air so she imagined him standing upright, as if an invisible platform were beneath him. She watched as his body turned into the position she wanted. He reached his hands up toward the top of the wall, grasping it as soon as he got close enough. She released the energy and allowed him to pull himself the rest of the way up. He looked down at her and gave her two thumbs up.

"Stosh first," she said up to him.

Stosh stepped toward the wall tentatively. "See you on the other side, Al."

Luke lifted him carefully and Ally watched as he disappeared over the top. Sabine went next, and then Willow. Asher stepped forward only after he spent a minute arguing with Ally that she would get to go next.

"I need to be here in case something happens. I can cover your back."

Asher had responded with, "Then who will protect yours?"

Luke. She thought to herself.

Asher was halfway up the wall when the Guards found them. Ally froze where she was, shocked by the sheer sight of them. A half-dozen of them appeared around the side of the house Ally and the others had been standing behind, their violet eyes glowing in the night. She gasped when she recognized the Guard leading the small ground. Pax grinned at Ally and then raised his gun, using it to shoot Asher out of the air.

Chapter Twenty-Five

A month ago, Ally would have fainted at the sight of a dead body at her feet. Now, well now the sight made her angry. It reminded her of the loss of her mother, and the loss of other Ordinarys at the mercy of the Exceptional Guards. She clenched her hands into fists at her side and looked up, watching as the Guards formed a line in front of her.

"We know what you're up to, Ally," Pax said. "Where are the others?"

Ally laughed, but it held no humor. "I'm by myself. Did you think they would want to risk coming with me?"

Pax shook his head. "Oh Ally. Did *you* think I didn't know about your friend, Willow? Luke sent Maver and I on a mission to find her two days ago, and then tonight she goes missing from her housing unit at the ORC. Doesn't that seem a little strange to you? And do you expect me to believe that you would leave your brother behind? So where are they? On the other side of the wall?"

Ally's body stiffened but she kept her expression calm.

One of the Guards with Pax coughed, and she recognized him as the Guard from the front gate her first day into the City.

"This can be easy, or this can be hard," Byron said.

"I think we'll go with hard," Luke said, appearing by Ally's side. He had jumped from above, falling two stories and landing on his feet.

Ally didn't waste any time. She raised her hands and found that the energy was still buzzing in her arms from when she had lifted Luke. She didn't hold back this time, not caring about the outcome of using her abilities this time. Hopefully she would blow the Exceptional Guards so far through the air that they would land several blocks mile away. She had never felt so much hatred for a group of people before, with the exception of Aden. But when the light from her hands directly met the three guards on the left, their bodies disintegrated into ashes. The other three Guards, including Pax and Byron, were thrown backwards.

Ally quickly dropped her hands to her side, managing to strangle the cry in her throat. "What have I done?"

Luke looked at her with horror filled eyes. "Ally." He reached toward her.

"No, don't touch me," she backed up.

"You had no choice," he said, continuing to move toward her.

"I killed them," she croaked, looking at her hands.

"Ally, you have to go." He motioned to the remaining Guards, who were starting to come to.

"What about you?" she said. "Come with us."

"I have to stay here." He took another step toward her. "I'll take care of them."

Luke raised his hands and her body lifted off the ground.

She took one last look at him, finally able to respond to his statement from earlier in the park. "I love you too, Luke."

"Stay safe, Ally. Come back to me." Luke said beneath her, but to this she had no response.

How could she ever return to this place? They would most likely kill her on the spot for murder. She wiped the tears from her eyes and looked up at the wall, grabbing the edge when she reached it. She lowered herself over the other side and quickly, but carefully, used the uneven stones as a way to climb down. On the ground, Stosh was pacing frantically.

"Ally!" he said, rushing to give her a hug once she was down safely. "We weren't sure what happened. We heard the commotion on the other side."

"You should have run!" she said, looking back toward the top of the wall. "We need to move. Now."

"What happened?" Sabine asked. "Where is Asher?"

Ally knew she didn't have time to be sensitive. "He's dead."

They ran toward the settlement but not directly into it. Ally didn't know if was adrenaline that kept them moving, or fear, but Stosh and Sabine made it with out stopping. Ally carried Willow over her shoulder and used her Exceptional senses to navigate them. They hid behind a large outcropping of trees for fifteen minutes, but saw no signs that the Guards were after them. Darkness had fallen over the woods, and the only sounds came from crickets and the night birds.

"We'll need to move quickly." Ally said to the others.

They left their hiding spot and began to run again. She led them right up to Po's house, hoping he was still awake. Stosh banged the door several times before leaning forward on his knees, making an attempt to catch his breath.

Po did finally come to the door and when he saw who stood on his porch, he almost fainted.

"Ally. Stosh. Willow," he said their names in a rush, his face turning white. "What's going on? What's happened? Where is your mother?"

Ally set Willow down. She took five minutes to give Po the extremely short version of what was happening, hoping that in the end he would believe her. She didn't know why she thought it would be as easy as marching into the settlement and getting everyone up and moving. Po seemed to be in disbelief that they were even here.

When she was finished, Po leaned against the wall, bringing his hand to his forehead. "I don't understand."

"You don't have to understand right now, but I can promise you that I'm telling the truth. Look at my eyes." She grabbed his face and forced him to look at her, making her violet eyes wide. "I'm an Exceptional now. We're leaving the settlement tonight and we need you to follow after us in a week. The Guards might come for us tonight, and we need you to tell them that you haven't seen us. They'll follow us into the Wilderness. We are going to lead them north; in the opposite direction I want you to go. We'll make sure we lose them before we head south again, and we'll make an attempt to catch up with you."

"Where will we go?" Po asked.

Ally felt relief that he was finally taking her seriously.

"To the southern City," she said.

Po's eyes widened. "No one knows where the City is. It has only been talked about in stories and we can't even be sure it ever existed."

"It exists, and you will find it. We all will," she said, placing a hand on either one of his shoulders.

THEY LEFT PO to think over her words, stepping out onto the dirt road that cut through the main part of town. Ally looked around, taking in the settlement. She had grown up here, and now it was barely recognizable. She had become so accustomed to the busy City, and the large buildings within it, that the settlement seemed small and fragile.

Sabine had a look on her face that Ally was sure that she herself had on her first day in the City, and Ally couldn't help but laugh. "Welcome to our home, Sabine."

Sabine smiled. "I kind of like it. Too bad we have to leave it behind."

"Let's gather more supplies from our house." Stosh said. "We'll need them if we want to make it in the Wilderness."

"How will we bring enough food?" Sabine asked.

Stosh laughed. "Out here, we get the majority of our food from the woods. We were born to survive in the Wilderness."

He took Sabine's hand in his and smiled. They went to Stosh and Ally's house, or *old* house now, dragging Willow behind them. She still hadn't spoken a word since they took her from the home, but she at least seemed to be coming out of her drug induced fog. Ally hoped she would be fully aware once it was time for them to leave. They couldn't leave her here to travel with the others. The Exceptional Guards would recognize her and take back to the City. They would then use her to get information on where Ally and the others had gone.

"I'll be right back. There is something I need to do," Ally said as the others quietly raided her old home. The family that lived with them previously had vacated the home, most likely after Guards had raided it to retrieve Stosh and their mother.

Ally left before they could respond and took the path behind their house that led into the woods. There were a few smaller homes back here, saved for single occupants, mainly the elderly. She found the home she was looking for and knocked on the door.

It took him a few minutes, but the man she sought after finally answered the door.

"Allona!" He said, inviting her in.

He was old, probably one of the oldest Ordinarys in their settlement, and definitely the friendliest. She sat in one of his worn, wooden rocking chairs and leaned back.

"So, am I old enough to know your name now?" She grinned.

Even her mother hadn't known his name, and they had been coming here twice a year for as long as Ally could remember. He would always joke, "When you're older" but of course, her mother had been much older than Ally.

The old man laughed, his eyes meeting hers. "I see the change has started. Have you come for another injection?"

"Will it reverse what is happening to me?" she asked.

He nodded. "It will, and if you want your symptoms to stay away, you'll have to keep up with the injections."

She filled him in on how the rest of the settlement would be leaving in a week's time and he grinned. "Finally, something exciting is happening around here. It is about time we stood up and thought for ourselves."

"So, you'll go?" Ally asked.

"Of course."

"I was wondering, could I take a shot or two with me into the Wilderness, just in case. I want to stay Exceptional for now, in case I need my abilities to help us, but if I change my mind—"

The old man smiled, hobbling over to a wooden chest near the fireplace. He opened it and pulled out half a dozen small, canvas bags. Each held a vial of the vaccine and the needle to administer it. He hobbled back and handed it to her.

"Here you go. I'll give you a few extra just in case. But in my opinion, Allona, you have always been able to do great things with out being Exceptional."

"Thanks, sir," she said. She pushed herself out of the chair and walked over to the door, knowing that she needed to find the others and leave.

"Oh, and Allona," the old man added.

She turned. "Yes?"

"My name is Kemp."

WHEN ALLY RETURNED TO HER HOUSE, Stosh, Sabine, and Willow were all waiting. Willow's eyes were looking less glazed over and she even smiled when she saw Ally.

"Are we ready?" Ally asked.

Stosh nodded, handing her a pack. "As ready as we'll ever be."

They cut through town and entered the woods on the north side, taking one last look back at the settlement. Ally knelt down by a large oak tree that marked one of the four corners of their settlement. Ordinarys had been carving their names into it for centuries, and the trunk was crowded with the writing.

She pulled a knife from her pack and carved her mother's name into one of the few empty spaces she could find. "I'm sorry I couldn't save you mother."

Stosh came up beside her and put a hand on her shoulder. "Do you think the others will leave? Do you think they'll head south like you asked?"

Ally turned her back on the settlement and stepped into the woods. "I hope so, Stosh. I really hope so."

Epilogue

Luke watched as Pax and Byron stood and surveyed their surroundings. The third Guard, the one who had managed to escape being vaporized, still lay on the ground. Pax dropped to one knee and pressed his fingers against the fallen Guard's neck.

"Dead," he said before standing again.

Luke rushed forward and grabbed Pax by the front of his Guard uniform, pushing him roughly. "Did you have to shoot Asher?"

"I panicked," Pax responded, holding his hands up in the air. "You told me to make it convincing. He was just an Ordinary."

Luke looked back to where Asher's body still lay crumpled on the ground. His body was positioned in an awkward angle, and his eyes were still wide open, staring up at the night sky.

"He was a friend," Luke responded.

"What shall we tell your father?" Byron asked.

"This wasn't supposed to happen." Luke motioned to the carnage around them. "If I had any idea--"

"What's done is done." Byron strapped his gun to his back and stepped over the fallen Guard's body. "This is why I brought four of the lowest ranked Guards with us. I've been around long enough to know to prepare for the unexpected."

"I still don't understand why we had to do all of this," Pax said.

"If Ally thinks she is being followed, she'll flee to the Wilderness, and tonight. If she thought she made a clean getaway, she might have tried to come back for me. Or even stay and convince me to come with,"

Luke responded.

"Would you have?" Pax asked. "Gone with her, I mean."

Luke looked at the ground. "I didn't want to have a chance to find out."

"Your father will be furious," Pax pointed out.

"Untrue," a voice came from behind them.

Aden stepped out of the shadows and joined their group; four Guards following close behind him.

"Father." Luke tried to keep his voice calm.

"This was actually quite a clever idea," Aden said with a laugh. "Although I will miss the opportunities to use Ally's abilities to better our City."

"Are you going to go after her?" Luke asked.

Aden shook his head. "No, I think it is best that we let Ally and her little friends wander into the Wilderness. She was only a distraction. She *is* a distraction."

Aden motioned to a Guard behind him and the man stepped forward, a cylinder shaped device in his hand. Luke couldn't react fast enough, and before he could raise his arms, two of the Guards had him in a choke hold. The other Guard, and Byron, were holding down Pax.

"This will really be for the best, Luke," his father said. "Tomorrow you will wake up with no recollection of Ally, and in turn, she will no longer be here to produce any reminders."

"Don't do this." Luke struggled against the Guards holding him.

"You've already let her go physically," his father smirked. "Let me help you with the mental part."

The Guard holding the memory-swiping device stepped over to Pax, who was also struggling against the Guards, and pressed the device up against the side of his head. He entered some information into the side and pressed a green button. The device let out a high-pitched whine and a bright flash of light emitted from the end touching Pax's temple. Luke watched as his best friend slumped to the ground, unconscious.

The Guard approached Luke next.

"Don't worry Luke, you'll remember the important parts of the last month, just not the parts that include Ally. She'll be but a shadow in your memories."

"One day," Luke spat. "I'll remember, and I'll hate you for this."

Aden just shrugged and turned his back, leaving Luke alone with the Guards. The device pressed into the side of his head, and he listened as information was entered into the controls. He squeezed his eyes shut and thought silently.

I will not forget you, Ally.

I will remember

I will remember.

There was a flash of bright light, and then darkness.

ACKNOWLEDGEMENTS

I wouldn't even be writing these words if it weren't for my dear friend Andrea, who urged me to push myself in my writing and move forward with my ideas. Thank you for reading each and every draft and revision, and giving me your open and honest opinions. To Alexis, for helping to edit my final drafts, and putting up with my constant questions and doubts. And for sharing in my GIF obsession when we both needed something other than writing to talk about. To BoSh, for being there for me through the ups and downs of the writing process, and for pushing me this far. To my husband and children, for putting up with me during this long and tiring process. Maybe now I'll find some time to do the dishes.

ABOUT THE AUTHOR

Jess Petosa is a Philly girl transplanted to the middle of Amish Indiana. Somewhere in between chasing two toddlers and meeting her one hundred books a year reading goal, she writes young adult fiction.

This is the first book in the Exceptional series. You can expect the second book to be available in late 2012 or early 2013. You can check her blog for more updates.

http://jesspetosa.blogspot.com

Made in the USA
Lexington, KY
29 April 2012